The River Girl's Christmas

Angela Castillo

ISBN: 1535358645
ISBN-13: 978-1535358644

To all those who love Christmas

Author's Note

In 1892, Christmas was becoming more celebrated, even in rural small-town Texas. The Christmas tree was set up in most homes, and shop windows beckoned people in with colorful displays of the latest toys and fashions. Churches hosted live nativity scenes, sometimes with real farm animals. It is my hope that this little story will take the reader to a simpler Christmas, a holiday season where family and faith shine brighter than shopping mayhem.

1

PRACTICE

*"Hark, the Herald Angels sing,
Glory, to the newborn King."*

Five angels in flour-sack robes sang with gusto as a trio of boys dressed in burlap costumes trembled on a stage built with wooden boxes.

"All right, Jonathan." Zillia clapped her hands for attention and Mrs. Fowler stopped playing piano. "The shepherds were afraid, not making faces. And Howard, please try to keep your finger out of your nose during the play."

"Yes, Mrs. Eckhart," the boys chanted in unison.

Zillia's five-year-old brother, Orrie, peered out from his burlap head covering. "How am I doing, Zilly?"

Zillia smiled. "You're a wonderful shepherd, Orrie. Try to act a little more surprised next time."

Orrie wrinkled his nose. "How can I be surprised when I know what's going to happen?"

"That's why it's called pretending, dear."

"Mrs. Eckhart, could you please help me with my costume?" Sadie walked up and turned around. Her robe, fashioned from an old curtain, gaped in the back where the pins had come undone.

"Of course, Sadie." Zillia rolled her eyes. Sadie always managed have a mishap of some sort. So far she'd stained her costume, tripped on the stage, and—worst of all, kept dropping the doll that served for Baby Jesus. *I'm glad Margo is too big and wiggly to play Baby Jesus. Not that I'd allow Sadie to carry her around anyway.*

Sadie flashed a sweet smile, the feature that had won her the part of Mary. "Thank you, Mrs. Eckhart."

Zillia nodded to Mrs. Fowler and the music started up again. The angels finished a rousing chorus of *Angels We Have Heard on High,* and then filed off the stage. Little girls giggled and boys jostled one another until they passed by Zillia's pew.

I'm glad I agreed to help Mrs. Fowler with the play this year. Zillia smiled. She'd participated in the Bastrop Methodist Church Christmas play when she was a little girl. Being in the play was one of the best parts of Christmas. She'd loved coming to church at night when the sky was still and dark. Every year she'd been an angel in the choir. Even though many of the children sang off key–and some even sang the wrong words–she'd always felt the play was important, like Christmas wouldn't be properly finished without it. Of course, that had been years ago. She was a married woman now.

A baby's cry broke into her thoughts. Zillia swiveled in her pew to see her husband, Wylder, come through the church door with their daughter in his arms. His blue eyes softened when he saw her, like they always did.

"Children, get ready for the manger scene," Zillia called over her shoulder as she went to meet him.

"Sorry, she was getting fussy." Wylder stroked Margo's pink cheek. "But we had a good day. We bought feed for the month, ordered the part for the thresher, and she picked out a new hair ribbon." He pointed to eleven-month-old's chubby fist, which clutched a rather bedraggled scrap of satin. "It's been a big day. But then we both decided we missed you."

Zillia laughed. "I've been gone half an hour. I think you could've survived."

"No, no, we couldn't." Wylder looked down at the baby. "Could we, Margo?"

Margo turned a tear-streaked face up to Zillia. She had stopped crying, but her tiny lip quivered.

"Oh my goodness, you poor little thing. You really are pining away, aren't you?" Zillia folded her daughter into her arms. "I suppose your father will have to run the play for me."

Wylder glanced over at the stage. Two of the three kings were competing to see who could stand on one foot the longest and Mary and Joseph leaned over the manger, poking at the baby doll. "Maybe you'd better stick with it. I've never been any good at this sort of thing. Remember when we spoke pieces in school?"

"And you could never get past the first line of the Declaration of Independence?" Zillia laughed. "You're right. At least stay and help corral the children who straggle off."

Wylder tucked back a straggling wisp of brown hair into his wife's bun. "I am pretty good at rounding up strays. I caught you, didn't I?"

"Wylder Eckhart, you shouldn't say such things in the house of the Lord." Zillia teased. She balanced Margo on one hip and went back to the stage. "All right, everyone. Shall we continue?"

Sadie looked up. "Mrs. Eckhart, we have a question. Did Baby Jesus spit up? My little brother spit up all the time when he was a baby."

"Margo did that when she was newly born." Orrie's eyes widened.

Zillia sighed. "Sadie, I don't think we should worry about that. Let's try to get through the play for now."

One of Wylder's eyebrows arched. "It's a good question. Did Baby Jesus spit up? I bet he did."

Zillia handed Margo back to him. "Take this child out of here and let me finish my play!"

Wylder grinned. "Sure thing." He headed back towards the church door. "Hope you can keep them from stampeding!" he called over his shoulder.

After practice, Zillia loaded a box of crooked halos and costumes that needed mending into the wagon. Beside this she placed a basket of food Mrs. Fowler had asked her to take to an ailing woman who lived on the way home.

Wylder brought Margo over from the porch. "Are you ready to load up?"

"Could you please find Orrie for me?" Zillia craned her neck over the edge of the wagon, looking for a glimpse of her brother's blond curls. "I would like to check in at the post office. I'm expecting that package from Grandma Rose."

"Oh yes, she's supposed to send you that dress for Margo," said Wylder. "I'll get everyone ready."

Main Street was just around the corner from the church. Rows of brick and wooden buildings lined the lane. Windows glowed with candles, paper chains and evergreen boughs.

Zillia stepped into the post office. Mr. Miller looked up from the counter, where he was sorting letters.

"Anything for me from Virginia?" Zillia asked.

"Nope, nothing. Sorry, Zillia. But I do have a letter for Wylder's grandmother. From the Oklahoma territory." Mr. Miller adjusted his wire-rimmed spectacles and rifled through a stack of papers on the counter. "Ah, here it is. Came in today."

Zillia took it and turned it over. "It's from Soonie. Thank you, Mr. Miller. I'll get this to Grandma Louise right away."

She ran over to the wagon and squeezed into the back with Orrie and Margo. "Wylder, Grandma Louise got a letter from Soonie! Could we please take it over on our way home?" She tucked her shawl around Margo's shoulders. A nip had crept into the afternoon air during practice.

Wylder's lips twitched and he stared down at his hands. "Of course," he said in the gruff voice he always used now when he spoke of his sister. "I'm anxious to hear what's going on with her as well. But don't we have to run an errand for Mrs. Fowler? I still have chores."

"Yes, the food for Mrs. Barnes. But her house is on the way. The stop won't take very long."

Wylder slapped the reins across the old mare's back and she plodded down the road that led out of town.

###

Zillia rapped on the door and stepped back, almost tripping down the broken porch steps. The windows of the house were dark, like soulless eyes guarding the road.

"I don't think anyone's home," she called out to Wylder, who watched her from the front seat of the cart.

Wylder's forehead wrinkled. "Mrs. Barnes should be home. She's doing poorly, so I don't know how she'd be anywhere else."

"Come on, Zilly!" Orrie yelled from the back of the wagon. "Margo looks like she's 'bout to wake up any second."

It's a wonder she ever sleeps with all the shouting that goes on. As Zillia reached up to knock again, the tarnished brass doorknob turned and the door swung open. A white-faced little girl peered out around the edge. "Hello?"

Zillia blinked. *I was sure Mrs. Barnes lived alone.* "Hello, I brought something for Mrs. Barnes. Is she here?" The child pushed her head a bit further through the doorway. Dark red hair hung in long strings around her face, dirty and unkempt. Her clothes weren't much more than rags, and smudges of dirt covered all visible skin. But her eyes shone like the first bluebonnets of spring. "Hi. Granny's here, but she can't get up right now."

"So she's your grandma?"

The little girl nodded. "Mama sent me here a few days ago. She said Granny could take one of us kids since she's got another baby. I came over with a wagon load from Smithville and Granny fetched me from town, but then she took ill. So I've been helping."

"You . . . what's your name? How old are you?" was all Zillia could think to say.

"Patsy. Patsy Locks. I'm seven last September. Did you bring something to eat?" The little girl stared at the basket in Zillia's hands with hungry eyes.

"I sure did. May I come in? I can put it on the table for you." Zillia turned and waved to Wylder. "I'll be back in a minute, dear."

Wylder shrugged and nodded.

Orrie scowled behind Wylder's shoulder.

Patsy swung the door open and Zillia stepped into the tiny room. Like several of the older houses in the area, the cabin consisted of one room, with a stove and table on one side, a fireplace and two chairs in a corner, and a bed in the other. An old woman slept in the bed. The stained quilt that covered her rose and fell with each snore.

The unmistakable stench of sickness filled the room and made Zillia's eyes water. She couldn't help wrinkling her nose.

"I'm sorry." Patsy lowered her eyes. "I've tried to clean things the best I can."

"Of course you have." Zillia gave the brightest smile she could muster. "Shall we see what the pastor's wife put in this basket?"

"Yes, please." Patsy bounced on her toes. "I'm so hungry."

Zillia began to clear a spot on the table. Dust coated the rough-hewn wood. Dishes, covered in moldy food, were stacked in piles. *Mrs. Barnes can't be much for housekeeping, even when she's well. Or perhaps she can't get around enough to clean.* Why hadn't the elderly woman asked the ladies of the church for help? Maybe she was too proud to ask.

After dusting off the table as best she could, Zillia opened the basket. The heavenly scents of gingerbread cookies and hot soup drifted through the room, masking the more unpleasant odors. "Mrs. Fowler said Mrs. Barnes might need a taste of Christmas, so she sent some of her best cookies." Zillia lifted out a round, warm sample.

Patsy clapped her hands. "They look so good. May I have one?"

"As soon as you go wash those hands."

While the little girl went outside to use the pump, Zillia moved over to the bed and stared down at Mrs. Barnes. The woman hadn't stirred through the visit. She seemed to be breathing evenly and when Zillia felt her forehead, it was cool to the touch.

She must be recovering from whatever's ailed her. Zillia breathed a sigh of relief.

Mrs. Barnes's eyelashes fluttered against her wrinkled cheeks and her eyes opened in slits. "Who–who are you?" she said in a weak voice.

"Zillia Eckhart, from church. The pastor's wife sent me over to bring food and check on you. I met your granddaughter. Looks like she's been a big help."

"Don't need your charity." The old woman spat the words through rotten teeth. She rolled over and faced the wall.

Patsy rushed in, drying her hands on her skirts, and snatched the cookie Zillia had set out for her. She carried it over to the farthest corner of the room and nibbled it, watching through slitted eyes, as though Zillia might decide to take it back.

Zillia regarded the filth and disarray. "Mrs. Barnes, I don't see any other food in here. Do you have enough to eat? We had a good harvest this year. I could bring preserves, bread and goat cheese if you'll handle it."

Mrs. Barnes rolled to face her again and propped herself up on one elbow, the yellowed ribbons on her nightcap quivering. "I— told you, we don't need no help. I'd ask you to take leave of my home." She lay back down and closed her eyes.

The front door opened a crack, and Wylder poked his head inside. "Zillia, Margo is fussing. We probably ought to head home."

"I'm coming."

He nodded and closed the door behind him.

Zillia went to the door.

Patsy followed her, her eyes widening. "I'm sorry, ma'am," she said in a low voice. "I think Granny's fractious because she's sick."

'Don't fret." Zillia opened the door and pointed to the road. 'See that path over yonder?"

The little girl nodded.

"If you need anything, just follow that lane around two bends. Right, then left. You'll see a giant oak tree, and a log fence. The first cabin is ours, all right?"

"All right."

Zillia felt the little girl's eyes follow her all the way to the wagon. A tear slipped down her cheek. She knew what it was like to feel hopeless and hungry. *I'll talk to Mrs. Fowler. Perhaps she can get Mrs. Barnes to accept help. Especially since Patsy is there.*

2

NEWS

Grandma Louise snatched the letter from Zillia's fingers. "You haven't opened it yet? How could you stand the suspense?"

"We had to wait for you, of course." Zillia placed Margo on the floor where a blanket had been spread. The little girl picked up her favorite toy, a wooden spoon, and waved it around.

Everyone, including Grandpa Walt and Wylder's cousins, Henry and Will, had gathered in the large front room that served for a kitchen and family room.

Eight-year-old Will bounced on his toes. "Hurry, please. We want to know about Soonie."

"Give me a moment. Let me sit." Grandma Louise settled into her ornately carved rocking chair, brought all the way from

Sweden. The chair tipped backwards, brushing the branches of the small pine tree brought into the house for the holiday.

Adjusting her spectacles, Grandma Louise unfolded the paper and cleared her throat. "Dear Family, I know you are all gathered around and listening, so let me first say I love you all and miss you dearly."

Orrie gasped as he sat down by Grandma's elbow. "It's like she can see us!"

"It is, isn't it?" Grandma Louise smiled. She continued to read.

"I told you in my last letter that Lone Warrior and I moved to the reservation in Fort Sill in July. We had received word from Uncle Isak that Hal, the evil man who caused us so much trouble, had died of blood poisoning. I wouldn't wish death on anyone, but we were so glad we didn't have to stay in hiding anymore. The schoolteacher who had been serving at the reservation moved on to another town. Lone Warrior felt a need to return to the reservation, and I was happy to be among my people once more. We have been here for several months now, and it has been wonderful to see everyone again, though life on the reservation isn't always easy."

"It's got to be better than sleeping on rocks in the wilderness," Wylder muttered.

Zillia nudged him with her elbow.

Grandma Louise raised her eyebrows but went on.

"Now for my happy news. Because of his work with the peace-keeping units at Fort Sill, my husband has received permission to travel into Texas. This means we can come down to Bastrop legally, without trouble from the law. Yes, everyone, we are coming for Christmas.'"

The room erupted. Orrie found a pie plate and beat it with a toasting fork. Henry and Will broke into a Comanche battle song, their bare feet slapping against the floor as they stomped to the rhythm.

Margo stared at them all and began to wail.

Grown woman that she was, Zillia was tempted to join the boys. *My best friend will be home.* Everyone in the family, had come to terms with the notion they might not see the sweet, spirited girl again.

Grandpa Walt lifted a leathered hand, and the hubbub died down. "Does it say exactly when they're coming?"

Grandma Louise scanned the last page of the letter. "Let's see here. They planned to get started with the journey on the 18th or 19th, so that would have been one or two days ago. She said they were going mostly by train, since they'd saved some money back from Lone Warrior's pay." Grandma looked up. "She thought they'd be here by the 21st or 22nd."

"So they will make it in time?" Zillia clasped her hands.

"Sounds like it." Grandpa Walt crossed his arms and leaned back in his chair; his suspenders strained almost to bursting with the stretch. "We got some stuff to get done."

"Let me handle the cooking and cleaning," said Grandma Louise. "You can finish up that bed you've been putting together for the spare room."

Wylder's grandparents had spent the summer and part of the fall fixing up a long unused room in the house. Zillia had wondered what guests they expected, but now seeing the look in Grandma Louise's eyes she knew–they'd held onto the hope that someday their granddaughter would return. Soonie had always slept in the small loft overhead, but of course she and her husband would need a bigger space.

So strange to think of her as married–and to someone I've never even met. But Soonie's letters had been filled with praises for the young Kiowa man she had fallen in love with, and Zillia had no reason to doubt he was every bit as wonderful as she described.

The boys and Wylder went outside to play some game they had invented with a ball and a stick, and Grandpa Walt ambled along to 'supervise.'

"Want me to start the dishes?" Zillia asked Grandma Louise, who rocked in her chair with the letter folded in her hands.

"Ah, sit with me a while first. The dishes will keep." Grandma Louise gazed at the Christmas tree, which Wylder had carried in that afternoon. The ornaments, carved by Wylder and Grandpa Walt over the years, still sat in a hatbox beside the tree, along with the fragile pressed-paper stars Grandma Louise had brought from

Sweden forty years ago when they traveled across the sea and then thousands of miles by land to Texas.

"It will be Margo's first Christmas tree." Zillia stroked the child's soft brown curls.

Grandma Louise smiled. "I wish you could have seen how we celebrated Christmas in the old country. Such a feast we had! Lutfisk and smoked pork and round towers of golden bread with a plum on top. One for each person. And there would be a knock on the door, and the Yule Goat would be there, with presents for everyone."

"What was the Yule Goat?" asked Zillia.

"Oh, it was kind of like Saint Nicolas. A goat man who brought presents to good girls and boys. My uncles would take turns dressing up in a costume my grandmother had made. It was a bit frightening, but we all knew it meant candies and gifts. After everything had been handed out, we would dance and sing. Oh!" Grandma Louise clasped her hands together. "The boys would love it."

"We have a nice Christmas here too," Zillia reminded her.

"Oh yes, of course we do, but I wish I had learned more of my mother's recipes before we left home. She died before I was old enough to watch her, and after that my father hired a fussy old cook who wouldn't allow me in the kitchen. I didn't learn to cook so well until I was married, and by then we were here, in this country, and I made Texas food." Grandma Louise sighed.

Zillia sat up straight, and the baby stirred in her arms. "What will we do for Soonie and Lone Warrior for Christmas? There's only five days! We don't have time to make anything. I suppose we could buy them something at the store. But store-bought isn't as special." Zillia tapped her finger against her lip. "I've been sewing an apron for myself. If I stay up late the next few nights, I could probably finish it for Soonie. I'm trimming it with lace from one of my mother's old dresses."

Grandma Louise stared into the fire, her faded blue eyes glistening. "I have something," she said softly. Holding up a wrinkled hand, she slipped off the garnet ring that was always there, even when she kneaded dough and washed dishes. The red stone winked in the firelight. "Grandpa Walt worked and saved for this ring for a whole year in Sweden. It's my wedding ring. I was going to give this to Soonie on her wedding day. But I didn't get a chance . . ." She choked and put her hand over her face.

Zillia put her hand on the elderly woman's shoulder. "But now you will. And it'll be even better, because it's Christmas."

"You're right, my dear." Grandma Louise removed her spectacles and wiped her eyes with her apron. "I need to be thanking the good Lord I get a chance to see my girl, even though the time may be short."

Zillia leaned back in her chair to cuddle her daughter and savor the rhythmic breathing of the sleeping child. "I wonder what we could make for Lone Warrior. I've never met a Kiowa person in my life. I'm not sure if they even celebrate Christmas."

Grandma Louise rose from her chair, went to the table, and began to clear dishes. "He probably wants the same things as any other man. A full belly and all the time in the world to hunt. And no farm chores ever again."

3

DANGER ON THE TRAIL

"Where you folks headed?" The buggy driver climbed down from his rickety perch, never taking his eyes off of Lone Warrior.

"We need to get to a livery stable owned by a Mr. Bollen. Do you know the place?" Lone Warrior craned his neck down to return the man's cold stare.

Soonie twisted her hands beneath her shawl. Lone Warrior wore the same type of suit a man would wear in any Texas town, with his long, black braids tucked under his broad-brimmed hat. But at half a head taller than most men and with the rich dark skin of his people, her handsome husband stood out.

"Yeah, I know the place. S'over by the Cedar Post hotel." The driver worked a chaw of tobacco from one cheek to the other, a thin stream of brown juice trickling from the corner of his mouth. He wiped his lips with his sleeve. "But I'm not sure I want savages in my buggy."

"I've got my letter of permission right here." Lone Warrior kept his voice even, though a muscle in his cheek twitched. "And I'm willing to pay extra." He pulled out a paper from his breast pocket and handed it to the driver.

The man unfolded the papers and examined them. "Fort Sill, huh?" He held up the coins Lone Warrior handed him and held them up in the light. "All right then." Swinging the buggy door open, he gestured for them to get inside. "But you'd better not dirty up my cushions."

Soonie dusted off the filthy seat before sitting on the very edge. "As if we could," she said to Lone Warrior in a low voice.

Lone Warrior sat back on the other seat, his features as calm as ever.

After a short, bumpy ride, the buggy stopped in front of a sprawling log cabin. Several horses grazed in the yard, and a man sat under the awning in a rocking chair.

Soonie had barely pulled her skirts free before the buggy jolted forward and away in a clatter of hooves and a screech of springs.

"Good thing I grabbed our things first." Lone Warrior held up their saddlebags.

The man on the porch stood up, stretched, and clambered down the steps. "Hello, you must be the folks from Oklahoma. I'm Mr. Bollen." He grasped Lone Warrior's hand and shook it.

"Nice to meet you," said Soonie.

Though Mr. Bollen had bushy black eyebrows and a beard that covered most of his face, his eyes twinkled from within the depths. "I think these two mares will do well for you," he said, leading Soonie and Lone Warrior to the paddock and indicating two horses tied to posts, already saddled and bridled. "They're sisters with Morgan blood. They might be small, but they have speed and stamina. They'll get you to Bastrop in no time."

Lone Warrior ran his hands over the dark bay's forelegs. He nodded. "They're perfect. Thank you so much."

Mr. Bollen handed the reins to Lone Warrior. "Captain Wilkenson spoke well of you two. He assured me you would bring them back without a scratch."

Soonie patted the sorrel mare's neck. "We will care for them as if they were our own." She and Lone Warrior had only left Fort Gill five days before, but already she missed her own horse, Stone Brother. She'd begged Molly to give him extra oats and carrots while they were gone.

"I'm sure you will." Mr. Bollen smiled, and his cheeks shone like red plums from beneath his whiskers.

Lone Warrior took two coins from his jacket pocket and handed them to the stable owner. "Thank you kindly." He slung their bags behind the saddles, and then gave one set of reins to Soonie. They led the horses through the paddock gates.

"I'm thankful to be riding a horse instead of a train," Soonie said to Lone Warrior as she climbed up in the saddle and arranged herself. Though she wore a calico 'white woman's' dress, she had her trusty doeskin breeches on underneath, which would make the day's journey much more bearable. Like many Texas women, she refused to ride side-saddle.

"Do you think your family got the telegraph?" asked Lone Warrior as they set off down the trail.

"I hope so. The man who runs Bastrop's post office is forever going out of town for family members' funerals—or that's what he says. And he's the only one who knows how to work the telegraph device. If he's not there, then hopefully they got the letter, at least." Soonie shivered. "Oh, I'm so excited to see everyone! And I can't wait for them all to meet you!"

"I just wonder if they will be as happy to see me." Lone Warrior said in a voice so low Soonie barely caught the words.

"What? Why wouldn't they? You saved my life more than once. You're my husband. You have every right to come and visit!"

"Yes, but I was also the one who took you away from them. You could have had a normal life, married a white farmer and stayed close to home."

Soonie rode close enough to touch his shoulder. "I've told you; my family isn't like that. They trust me, Lone Warrior. If I am happy, they will be happy."

Lone Warrior shrugged. "Even so, change can be difficult for some people."

"You will have to sleep in a white man's house instead of a tipi for a few days," Soonie teased. "Do you think you can handle that?"

"I slept in a boarding house and on the train," Lone Warrior's tone was serious. "Stuffy, hot places, with thick walls." He glanced down at her and smiled. "I will do it . . . but only for you."

Soonie's heart beat a little faster. Even after being married for almost a year, she still melted every time her husband gave her that special smile.

After they'd left the small settlement and escaped from Hal, they had spent months living in the wild places of Oklahoma. Most of their time had been spent hunting and foraging for food. On rare days they'd gone hungry, though with Lone Warrior's hunting skills, those times had been few. Many nights they'd huddled in caves or shelters built of sticks, too cold to sleep. But Soonie never regretted her choice to follow her true love. She'd do it all over again if he asked.

After a few hours, they stopped in Del Valle, a tiny town consisting of a cluster of homes and a combination post office-general store.

"We can wash up at the pump by the store and eat our lunch under that tree." Soonie pointed to a shady place.

Lone Warrior shook his head. "I don't think that's a good idea. Someone might see us and get suspicious."

After scanning the area, Soonie shrugged. "I don't see anyone out. Besides, this is where I always met Uncle Isak when he brought things to trade. No one ever bothered us here. Of course, I didn't realize at the time how much he was risking by choosing to meet with us."

Lone Warrior squinted at the trading post. "Is there a river or stream somewhere ahead?"

"Yes, in maybe half an hour."

"We'll go there." He urged his horse forward.

Soonie bit back a protest. She had learned to trust her husband's instincts in these situations. If she had brought up similar concerns, she knew he would have valued her thoughts as well.

The brook was just where Soonie remembered it and the water was cold, clear and clean. After a lunch of bread and cheese, Lone Warrior took a quick nap on a large, flat rock in the watery December light.

After half an hour, Soonie shook him awake. "We probably ought to get going, dear. We have at least two hours of riding ahead of us, if we don't make any more stops."

Lone Warrior pushed back his hat, which had been covering his face, and yawned. "All right." He peered up at the sun. "Two hours, you say? We should make it by dark."

The ride was pleasant enough, a mild winter day like many in Texas. Cardinals and other winter birds sang in the trees by the roadside, and a few hardy blue-black butterflies flitted among the dandelions, which always seemed to sprout in every season, except in times of rare snow.

As the shadows grew longer, the air chilled. Though Soonie didn't mind the cold, she wished she could snuggle in Lone Warrior's arms to get warm. She hadn't expected to miss the tipi they'd set up on the outer edge of the reservation, but now she longed to see the shadows dancing on the hide walls and the mysterious shapes the smoke made when it disappeared through the top.

Life on the reservation had been an adjustment. Due to her teaching position and Lone Warrior's job as head of the reservation patrol, they both had more freedoms and favor than many of the other Comanche and Kiowa people in the territory. She'd taken up teaching again, and she loved her pupils fiercely. But the prison-like atmosphere the reservation held could be stifling at times, and Soonie gulped the free air with gratitude.

Lone Warrior held up a dark, scarred hand and halted the bay.

"What is it?" Soonie asked, scanning the path.

He swung down off the horse and gestured for her to do the same.

"Did you see something? What's wrong?"

Grabbing her hand, he pulled her towards him. "Nothing. Just this." He reached down, and his lips found hers.

She kissed him back and pulled away, gasping and laughing. "Silly man! We have to reach town. It's going to be black as pitch soon. Good thing they'd have had time to finish building that bridge across the river. We'd never wake the ferry man at this hour."

"Sorry, I couldn't wait any longer." Lone Warrior touched her face. "Those lips just kept taunting me."

The rattling of wheels interrupted their embrace.

Lone Warrior shielded his eyes and looked down the path. "We should get off the road."

"Don't be silly." Soonie patted his arm. "We're only a few miles from Bastrop. Everyone around here knows me."

Lone Warrior stiffened and stepped in front of her as a buggy appeared around the corner.

Two men Soonie didn't recognize sat in the front, and a third man rode behind on a horse.

"Whoa, whoa." The driver pulled up the reins. The wagon came to a stop a few feet away from Soonie and Lone Warrior.

26

The driver was tall and lanky, with a drooping black moustache and a bowler hat. The other two men were also dark, but more plainly dressed.

The driver squinted at Lone Warrior. "Howdy. What are you folks doing out here?"

"Visiting family for Christmas." Soonie straightened and lifted her chin. "How about you?" The hairs on her neck rose as rocks crunched behind them. The man on the horse now blocked any chance of escape.

"Say now." The driver slid down from his seat and walked towards them. "You must be part Injun, ain't you, girl? He peered under her bonnet. "I'd say Comanche. And you," he jabbed a finger at Lone Warrior, "I don't know what you are, but I'm thinkin' you're one hundred percent red man. Are you legal or illegal?"

"We're legal." A muscle in Lone Warrior's cheek twitched. He reached into his coat pocket, where their permission papers had been stored.

"Wait!" Soonie cried, but the shot rang through the air too fast for either of them to react. A spurt of red bloomed through a fresh hole in the fabric of Lone Warrior's coat. His hand flew to the wound and he staggered back.

Soonie threw her hands into the air. "No more shooting! He was just going to show you his permission papers, written and signed by General Wilkenson himself!" Her legs wobbled and she fought to stay lucid, to stay in control. *Losing composure will do nothing for us right now.*

The wagon driver nodded to the man on the horse, who placed his gun back in its holster.

"Shouldn't be out here, anyhow. I'd argue in a court of law that savage was going for his gun." He glanced at the other two men. "Right boys? You saw what happened."

The other two men nodded, murder burning in their eyes.

Lone Warrior clutched his arm, wobbling where he stood. Blood spurted through his fingers. "Leave us alone," he said through gritted teeth.

"Sure, we'll leave you all alone," the man with a mustache taunted. "In fact, we're taking these horses, too."

"They don't belong to us!" said Soonie.

"See, I had a feeling. Did ya' hear that, boys?" He pounded a gloved fist into his hand. "Trying to shoot our heads off, and horse thieves as well. Some things just never change." He grabbed the horse reins and tied them to the back of the wagon.

"No, we borrowed them. We have to give them back!" Soonie stepped forward, but Lone Warrior clutched her arm.

"No," he said, so quietly she could scarcely hear.

His face had turned from rich umber to a sickly gray, and blood flowed down his shoulder in a torrent.

The buggy creaked and the man clicked to his horses.

Soonie stepped towards the wagon. "You can't just leave us here without horses! My husband could bleed to death! Have you no hearts?"

The man on the horse turned and smirked. "One less Injun in this world."

The buggy and beasts disappeared in a cloud of dust.

Lone Warrior staggered a few steps, then stopped, his head hanging.

Soonie took his good arm. "You have to sit down. I must examine that wound."

She helped him over to a tree and he sank to the ground, easing against the trunk. "Come on, we have to get your coat off." She knelt in the dirt, ignoring the pine needles that dug into her knees through her breeches.

Lone Warrior's eyes were shut tight, his lips drawn in a grimace. "Do what you need to do. I don't think it's too bad."

Soonie slid her traveling satchel from her shoulder. She pulled a small knife from her belt and swiftly cut his shirt away. Blood streamed from a dime-sized hole in her husband's arm. She examined the other side. Trying to keep her voice from shaking, she said, "Here's the good thing. Bullet went right through. Let me get you bandaged up. Hopefully someone more helpful will come down this road in the next short bit. We used to have a good doctor in town, chances are he's still there."

She tried to keep her tone light and cheerful, but she'd helped her friend, Molly, with plenty of injuries. *I only have a few minutes to stop the blood flow. He could die right now.*

Pulling her canteen from her shoulder, she sent up a silent prayer of thanks she hadn't chosen to fasten it to her saddlebag instead. She poured the last of the lukewarm water over the wound. "All right, let me get this tied up. It will probably feel better."

"Of course it will," said Lone Warrior through clenched teeth. "Augh. If only I could have met those men on a battlefield. Cowards."

"Yes, they were. But right now we need to get you fixed up." Tearing strips from her petticoats, Soonie fashioned a quick, neat bandage. To her satisfaction, no blood seeped through the cloth.

"All right, my love. You stay here. I heard a stream a little way back, and I'm going to fetch more water."

Her husband nodded, and she went off through the trees.

The stream was nothing more than a silver trickle, but enough to serve her purpose. She dipped the canteen in, watching the hollow of water created by the mouth.

More wagon wheels from the road. And this was a heavier wagon. She grabbed the canteen and ran towards the lane.

A buckboard. A man was driving with a young woman beside him. A little boy, maybe five years old, sat in the back.

The woman swiveled back, caught sight of Soonie and gripped the man's arm. Blond hair wisped from beneath her smart straw bonnet. "Connor!" she shrieked.

I know her. "Claire!" Soonie cried out. "Claire Blakeman? It's me, Soonie. Remember? We went to school together."

"Oh, yes." Claire's brow furrowed.

Soonie glanced down at her blood-spattered, torn dress. *I look a fright.*

The man beside Claire frowned. "Do you know this woman?"

"Y-yes." Claire lowered her eyes. "It's been a long time."

The boy dangled his feet of the back of the wagon and stuck his tongue out at Soonie.

"Please," said Soonie. "My husband is hurt. If you could just give us a ride to town. He needs to see a doctor."

"Of course." Claire tapped her fingertips against her lips "Connor, could you go take a look?"

The man handed the reins to Claire and ambled down from the wagon.

"Oh, thank you so much!" Soonie beckoned for him to follow. "He's right under this tree."

Lone Warrior had slid down to the ground all the way now. His eyes were closed, and his head lolled to one side. His long braids twined around his shoulders like curled snakes.

"Oh." Connor stopped short. "I didn't realize . . ." He squinted at Soonie. "Ma'am, I was forgetting my horse, she's been acting a bit lame and I think the added weight might be too much for her to pull "

"I'll walk beside. Surely you can help me?"

Connor moved quickly back to the wagon and spoke to his wife in low tones Soonie couldn't understand.

Claire glanced back at Soonie, her lips pale and her face white. She nodded.

They aren't going to help. They're going to leave us here. Soonie felt as though her insides had plummeted to the ground.

"Please, please at least tell my folks were we are!" she shouted.

Conner gave a swift, firm shake of his head.

For the second time that day, she watched helplessly as the wagon rattled out of sight.

4

GRITS AND GRIT

Zillia squinted at the tiny lines of writing that wobbled over the yellowed paper. She'd managed to sneak Grandma Louise's recipe book from her pie safe, but she hadn't realized the recipes would be in Swedish.

"It's no use." She sighed and closed the book and turned back to her wash basin full of dishes.

Wylder came in, carrying Margo. "What's the matter?"

He sat the little girl in his lap and slid a tin plate close enough for her to reach it. "Eat your grits, sweetheart."

Zillia looked up and rolled her eyes. "Don't let her eat on her own, she makes such a mess."

"A little mess never hurt anyone." Wylder patted Margo on the head with an adoring smile. "She needs to eat some real food, not just milk all the time. Why, when I was her age, I could polish off a side of ham in five minutes flat."

I'm sure you could. Zillia opened the recipe book again.

Margo grabbed a handful of grits and spread the mush all over her face. The yellow, grainy substance dripped down her cheeks. She grabbed another handful and threw it at Wylder, who dodged the mush. The grits splatted on the wall beside him.

Wylder gave Zillia a slanted look and wiped Margo's face with a flour sack. He gestured to the recipe book. "I haven't seen that book in a while. Grandma never makes Swedish recipes. I suppose it's too hard for her to find the right ingredients here. Did you borrow that from her?"

"You could say that–only she doesn't know I took it," Zillia looked down at her hands. "I thought maybe I could find one of her recipes from Sweden and make something special for Christmas. She's always talking about how much she enjoyed the holiday when she was a little girl."

"Hmm." Wylder took the book with one hand, trying to hold it away from Margo as he examined the pages. "Can't help much there. I know more Comanche than Swedish. Maybe Grandpa could make out some of the words." He glanced up at her. "It's a nice idea, but even if you can get the recipe translated it might be too tricky to make. Especially considering your—ahem—past cooking adventures. Didn't you already make Grandma a present?"

"Yes, a scrapbook for all her letters and keepsakes. But I wish I could do something more. She does so much to help us."

Wylder balanced a glob of grits on the end of a spoon and poked it towards Margo. "Come on, sweetheart, just a little bite!"

Margo's pink lips parted and Wylder pushed in the spoon.

"See, they taste good."

A shower of grits flew through the air as Margo sprayed her father, her mother and most of the kitchen. She banged the table with her fist and laughed.

"Perhaps we can try the grits another day?" Zillia wiped off the recipe book and placed it on top of the kitchen hutch. She put her chin in her hands.

"Nonsense." Wylder scrubbed at his face and swooped in with another spoonful. His teasing smile turned into a frown. "I'm sure you'll figure out something nice for Grandma."

"It isn't that." Zillia attempted to smooth the worry lines on her forehead. "I've been thinking about Patsy, that little girl at Mrs. Barnes's house. She's only seven, too young to care for an invalid. And they didn't have enough food in the house to feed a gnat."

"I'm sure Mrs. Fowler will check in on them," said Wylder.

He doesn't know what it's like to go hungry. For years after Zillia's mother died, she'd cared for her baby brother on her own. She'd mostly been able to scrounge food for them, and kind neighbors and friends shared extra produce and meat. But a few times the last piece of bread or cupful of beans had gone to Orrie, and she'd been left with nothing but dreadful pangs gnawing at her innards.

"I think I'll call on Mrs. Fowler again tomorrow, if that's all right with you."

"Of course." Wylder stood up. Grits covered his shirt front and peppered his beard. "I think Margo's full now."

The baby laughed again. Her brown curls stood on end, stiff with the breakfast food.

"Maybe." Zillia sighed and swished the flour sack in her wash water. *I really didn't need any extra work this morning, and now I have to clean this up.*

The outside porch stairs creaked, and the door flew open. Orrie ran in, banging the door behind him.

"Orrie! Please don't slam the door. And don't forget to wipe your feet!"

"Sorry, Zillie." Her little brother looked back at the mud he'd tracked in and gave an apologetic smile. "I had to tell you about Soonie."

"Is she here? Did she come with you?" Zillia ran to the door and fumbled with the handle.

"No, no, but Grandpa Walt got a telegram from Austin. Soonie sent it yesterday morning."

"Austin?" Wylder came in from the bedroom and picked up his hat from the mantle. "They should be here by now." He frowned. "They should have been here last evening."

"It's still early," Zillia protested. "You haven't even started the milking yet. They probably decided to spend one last night in the open air before they got here."

"That's what Grandpa Walt said." Orrie grabbed a piece of cornbread from a platter on the table. "And Grandma said, 'Our girl would come home as fast as she could.' And Grandpa smiled all silly and said something about young love." Orrie wrinkled his nose. "That's when I left."

Zillia pursed her lips and looked over at Wylder.

He drew his eyebrows together. "Hey, Orrie, will you grab the milking pails and take them into the barn? I'll be right there."

"Sure." Orrie dashed back through the door, slamming it again.

Wylder put his hat on and came over to Zillia. He cupped her chin in his hand. "Don't worry. I'm sure they'll be all right. It's probably that Kiowa man. Maybe he decided to go off and raid some innocent travelers."

"Wylder Eckhart!" Zillia gasped. "How can you say such a thing? You're part Comanche yourself!"

"Yes, but you don't see me skulking out in the bushes and leading folks' sisters into danger." He opened the door. "I'm off to milk before the cows burst their udders."

Zillia closed the door after him and finished wiping the last traces of grits from Margo's face. She'd had no idea Wylder felt that strongly about Soonie marrying Lone Warrior. If anything, he'd seemed indifferent. She sighed. *I should know him better than that. We were friends for years before we got married. He's never been one to spout out his feelings easily.* But still, for him to make a personal remark about someone's heritage . . . he must be extremely upset.

As she swept the cabin floor, Zillia prayed for Soonie and Lone Warrior to arrive safely. And she prayed that Wylder's attitude would change. *I'm sure once they get home, everything will be fine.*

###

A twig tickled the back of Soonie's neck, and she brushed it away and sat up. First light filtered through the trees, washing over Lone Warrior, whose breaths came shallow and quick. A stand of evergreens shielded them from the road. A thick bed of leaves protected them from the moist, cold soil.

"Oh, I didn't mean to sleep." Soonie tugged the canteen down from the branch where it had been hanging and crawled to her husband's side.

Sweat beaded Lone Warrior's forehead, despite the cold December morning. She'd covered him with her woolen shawl and underskirt, but he still shivered.

All night she'd debated whether or not she should leave him and get help, but the danger was too great. A cougar or coyotes could be drawn by the scent of blood, or worse still, another treacherous human could find him and decide to finish the job. *How could people be so cruel? They know nothing about us.*

She patted his good shoulder until he opened his eyes. She let out a gusty sigh. "You're awake."

A weak smile tugged at one side of his mouth. "Good morning, my love."

"Good morning. Can you sit up? You need some water."

He lifted his head, but then rested it back down.

He's so much weaker than yesterday. She drizzled water into his mouth. Though most trickled down his cheek, he managed to swallow some. "Good. You need to keep drinking."

The men had taken most of their belongings along with the horses, including her flint and matches, so she'd had no way to start a fire. Somehow this didn't sting as much as the loss of the Christmas presents they'd brought from Oklahoma and her Bible. "We've got to make it to town somehow."

"Why?" Lone Warrior closed his eyes. "So someone can shoot me again?"

"Not everyone is like that here. We encountered the wrong people at the wrong time. Remember the man who rented us the horses? He was very kind."

"He's not going to be so happy when he finds out we can't return his beasts." Lone Warrior sighed.

"We can't think about that right now. I've got to figure out how to get you somewhere safe so I can make it to town for help. First thing I need to do is move you off the side of the road. No telling who's going to ride by. Though it's colder today, and I don't know if there'll be as many travelers. Do you think you can walk a little?"

Lone Warrior sighed. "My head aches." He gave a shaky laugh. "Some warrior I've turned out to be. In my life I've been stabbed, sliced by an axe and kicked by a horse. I've never felt this bad."

"Even though we stopped the flow, you lost a lot of blood. You're going to be weak for a while." Soonie walked around the edge of the road, testing the larger branches littering the ground. Most were rotten and brittle. A cluster of pine saplings caught her eye. She picked out two the thickness of her wrist, pulled out her knife and hacked them down. Stripping the branches from the trunks, she crossed the sticks at the tops to create an 'A' shape.

After a few moments of poking around, she found three sturdy sticks and lashed them to the poles with strips of cloth from her dress, like rungs of a ladder.

"I know it's cold, but I have to use the shawl. You're going to need some kind of padding." She took the cloth and spread it over the sticks.

"All right, let's get you on here." She pointed to her makeshift travois.

He raised his eyebrows. "I know you're strong, but can you really pull me on that?"

"We only need to go a short way. The bridge can't be far from here. And if we can't make it that far, we can at least get off the road a bit so we won't be attacked again." Tears stung the corners of her eyes. "Oh, Lone Warrior, I'm so sorry about this. I was the one who wanted to come. I know evil people can be found wherever we go, but I never thought something like this could happen near the town I love so much."

His hand crept up and settled on her arm. "Soonie, you have so much faith in people. You believed in me, even when I wasn't the best person. How can I be angry with you for the thing I love about you the most?"

"The worst part will be getting you on here. Might as well do it now." Soonie dragged the travois so it was parallel with her husband's body.

"I can manage a bit." Lone Warrior pushed himself up on his elbow. After quite a bit of tugging on Soonie's part and more than a few Kiowa words that weren't very nice, he was settled on the travois.

"Lord, give us the strength to get to where we need to be," Soonie prayed.

"Amen," said Lone Warrior.

"Hang on." Soonie pulled the knife from its sheath once more and surveyed the trees that faced the road. Choosing a stout cedar that twisted up from the ground, she carved a large bird in flight into the bark, with its beak pointed in the way she intended to go. She hacked a strip of blue lace from the hem of her skirt and tied it above the bird. *This will have to do. Hope Wylder comes looking for us.* As children. she and her brother had played a game where they took turns hiding in the woods, with only the little bird carvings to show where they went. *Of course he will. God, please help him to see it.*

Soonie stepped inside the upper frame of the travois and grabbed the top point. She hoisted the contraption to the level of her waist and pulled. The travois slid across the ground much more easily than she expected it to. "I can't see behind me, so you have to tell me if you're slipping."

"Yes. I know." Though she couldn't see her husband, she could tell he was speaking through gritted teeth.

Lifting her chin, she pressed through the trees. Staying off the main road and still finding smooth enough ground to drag her husband through without jostling him would be tricky.

"We have to be close to the bridge. If only we could get to town, I have many friends there. The doctor. Mr. and Mrs. Fowler. Sheriff Andrews. He was always kind to me."

"Sheriff Andrews, huh? How old is this sheriff?"

"My goodness, is that a hint of jealousy I hear?" Soonie set down the travois and stepped back. Her arms ached already.

Lone Warrior was smiling. "Just teasing. I have to do something to pass the time back here."

"Sorry I can't go any faster." Soonie picked up the sticks and began dragging them again.

"Don't talk crazy. I know you're going as fast as you can."

Soonie racked her brain for something else to talk about. "I wonder how Molly is doing, teaching the school."

"She probably decided to quit early for the holiday. I would have with the unruly bunch you teach."

She could hear the teasing in his voice again, and she knew he was doing it to keep her spirits up. The light tone had a tiny edge, a lace of pain that ran through it, urging her forward.

I will make it to town. And he will be fine. If only we can find friends to help us.

5

PATSY

"That's it." Wylder took a gulp of water, swirled it in his mouth, and spit it out on the ground. "I'm going out to look for them."

Zillia handed him two molasses cookies, fresh from the oven. "I'm glad you decided to go. I can't imagine what could be keeping them. Will Grandpa Walt be able to ride with you?"

"Yep." Grandpa Walt said as he rode through the front gate on his splendid chestnut mare, Ladybird. "Would have left sooner but Grandma Louise kept on about this fiddle-faddle with young love."

Didn't Orrie say Grandpa Walt had been the one talking about that? Zillia glanced over at Wylder and he gave her his lopsided smile.

"We should be back before supper, I reckon." Grandpa Walt's thick white eyebrows bristled under his hat. "I'm sure everything's fine. I'm thinking one of the horses threw a shoe or something like it.

"I'm thinking Soonie and her man will want to eat at our house when we get back. Zillia, Grandma told me to ask you to bring the children and spend the day, if you like."

"All right, we'll be right over." Zillia reached up and kissed Wylder on the cheek. "Please be careful."

"Of course." Wylder swung up into the saddle.

"Be nice," Zillia whispered, so only he could hear.

"Mmm hmmm." Wylder rolled his eyes. He clicked to his horse and the two riders moved off.

After packing up the cookies and a batch of spare cloth diapers, Zillia carried Margo to Grandma Louise's home with Orrie skipping beside her. The air was fresh and crisp, like the first bite of a winter apple. White clouds streaked the deep indigo sky, as though painted by giant fingers.

Grandma Louise came to the door, wiping her hands on an apron Zillia's mother had made years before. "Come in. We've lots to do for the next three days. Figured the busier we are the less worried we'll be."

The rich scent of pumpkin filled Zillia's senses as she stepped into the cozy home, along with mincemeat, cinnamon, and half a dozen other delightful holiday aromas.

Orrie stood in the middle of the kitchen and gave appreciative sniffs until Grandma Louise smacked him with a flour sack. "Go help Henry and Will. They're out back peeling apples."

"For pie? You bet!" Orrie ran through the back door.

The Christmas tree now boasted ornaments, strings of popcorn, and picture postcards sent over the years from Grandma Louise and Grandpa Walt's Swedish relatives. Grandpa Walt had positioned the tree in the same corner Zillia's parents had placed their tree when she was a little girl. A lump rose in Zillia's throat. *Will the ache ever go away? I still miss them so, so much.* It had made sense for Grandma and Grandpa to buy her parents' home and larger piece of land and for her and Wylder to move with Orrie to the smaller cabin after they'd been married, but it was still hard to come back sometimes, to see someone else's keepsakes and furniture and pictures replace the ones belonging to her family.

Even though really, we're all family now.

Farm dogs barked outside. Zillia raised her eyebrows at Grandma Louise "Could they be home already?"

"Dear Lord, please let it be!" Grandma hastily washed clumps of pie dough from her fingers.

A knock sounded at the door. "None of them would knock," Zillia sighed.

Sure enough, when Grandma Louise opened the door, Mrs. Fowler stepped in, her gray-brown locks perfectly arranged beneath a white straw bonnet. Though the wife of a Methodist preacher, she refused to wear the dowdy clothes considered fitting for a woman of her position. She'd been the subject of gossip circles when her husband had first taken the pulpit, but had soon won the cackling biddies over by her graciousness and willingness to serve.

"Good afternoon, everyone." Mrs. Fowler swept off a knitted shawl and hung it on a hook by the door. "I'm sorry to come by without notice, but I need help." She must have noticed the concern on the women's faces, because her eyes clouded with worry. "My goodness, whatever is the matter?"

"We're waiting for Soonie and her husband to get here." Grandma Louse dipped out a cup of apple cider from a pot on the back of the stove and handed the fragile porcelain teacup to the pastor's wife. "They were supposed to arrive last night. Wylder and Walt went looking for them about an hour ago."

"Well, I hope they're all right." Mrs. Fowler blew on her cider and took a small sip.

"I'm sure they will be," said Zillia. "Go ahead and tell us your errand, Mrs. Fowler." The Fowlers had stepped in for her and Orrie more than once when they had been in need, and she was willing to do just about anything in return.

"I went to take Mrs. Barnes some food today and saw the dreadful condition of the house." Mrs. Fowler wrinkled her nose.

"I was going to come to town later this afternoon and tell you about the situation," said Zillia. "How is the little girl?"

"She was crying when I got there, poor thing. Just a mite, and dirty as a pig farmer. I tried to rouse her grandma but couldn't wake her. I sent for the doctor. He said this sickness isn't usually so serious if a body has the right care, but because of the conditions she might not pull through."

Zillia bowed her head. "I should have come back into town that night to let you know. Only Mrs. Barnes was so insistent that I leave. I wasn't sure if she would accept our help. She was even angry about the food."

Mrs. Fowler patted her hand. "Don't blame yourself, dear. Mrs. Barnes has always been a proud, stubborn old soul. But she'll have to be helped now. We've moved her to a home in town and are using church funds to hire someone to be a nurse and housekeeper for the next few days to see if we can help the woman pull through. She isn't well enough to travel all the way to Austin to a hospital."

"What about Patsy?" Zillia asked.

"That's why I'm here. Pastor Fowler and I would have been happy to take her in for a time, but as you know, my daughter and her family have come for the holidays from San Antonio. We simply don't have anywhere for her to sleep. I realize you are expecting guests, Mrs. Eckhart. Zillia, perhaps she could stay with you and Wylder?"

Another child to manage? At least she's older and can pretty much care for herself. I'd hate to say yes without asking Wylder, but I'm sure he'd never turn away someone in need. And I can't object, not after knowing what it's like to be abandoned myself. Taking a deep breath, Zillia nodded. "She can sleep in Soonie's old room, to the side. It's tiny, but clean and cozy. It will certainly be better than where she lived before."

"All right then, it's settled. I left her outside with the boys." Mrs. Fowler set her now empty cider mug on the table and rose from her chair. "She's had lunch." She lowered her voice. "But she really needs a bath. And if you plan to stay here for the afternoon you will probably want to give her one before you take her home."

Zillia placed Margo on a blanket in the corner and gave her a spoon and a pan to play with. "I'll heat up some water."

"I appreciate the help. I'll let you know as soon as the old woman has recovered. In the meantime, I will try to contact her mother." Mrs. Fowler shook her head. "It's hard to believe any parent could leave their child in that terrible situation."

Zillia pressed her lips in a thin line. *Not when it's happened to you.*

The back door creaked open and Orrie came in, leading Patsy. Despite the children being two years apart Patsy wasn't much bigger than Orrie.

"I told Patsy she could have some cookies, and I thought there might be one for me," said Orrie, peeking under the towel covering the basket of baked goods Zillia had brought.

"You're right. Take these out to your cousins." Zillia handed three cookies to Orrie. "Skedaddle. I need to talk to Patsy."

"O.k." Orrie glanced over at Patsy. "Hurry up, though, you're supposed to show us how to whistle on that blade of grass."

"Course I will." Patsy smiled shyly.

"Good." Orrie ran back out the door with his precious cookies in his hands.

"Patsy, it's good to see you again," said Zillia, handing the little girl two cookies. Patsy took them and nibbled tiny bites from the edges. *She'd probably rather wolf them down but doesn't want to seem impolite. She's been taught some manners, anyway.*

The girl met Zillia's gaze with her blue, hollow eyes and Zillia looked away. *Poor little girl, don't want her to feel uneasy.* She'd experienced her share of stares and sympathetic smiles in her difficult years.

"I'm glad you two are already acquainted." Mrs. Fowler came over to the table. "And Patsy, this is Mrs. Eckhart."

"Call me Grandma Louise. Everyone else does."

The pot on the stove was steaming now.

"Patsy, how would you like to get cleaned up and have some fresh clothes to wear?" Zillia asked the little girl, who was picking the last few crumbs of cookie off the tablecloth.

The pinched face brightened. "A bath? Oh, it's been so long. Could I really have one today? Now?"

"Of course. But you'll have to wear boy's clothes. Just until we get home, then I'll get you something from the things I've put back for Margo when she's older."

The little girl pushed her long, stringy hair out of her eyes. "I don't mind at all. Wore Jimmy's clothes more n' once. Jimmy was my twin, you know, though I was older by an hour, my ma said."

"Where is Jimmy now?" asked Grandma Louise.

"Ma says he's in Heaven, but my older brother, Wade, said he's just in the church cemetery, since we were all at the funeral and we didn't see no angels coming down to take him to glory. Ma says they're invisible, but Wade said even if the angels can't be seen, we could see Jimmy right there, down in the coffin."

Patsy told this story in a cheerful tone, without a trace of sadness in her voice.

"Goodness," was all Zillia could think to say.

"Well of course he's in Heaven, dear," said Mrs. Fowler. "The reason you didn't see him go was because only his spirit went. A spirit is something human eyes can't see."

"Hmmm." Patsy looked doubtful.

Zillia lifted the pan from the stove. "Missy, this water is nice and hot. Let's get you back here and clean you up before supper."

Patsy followed her into the small washroom, where a clean wash tub, scrub brushes and soap awaited.

"I'll pour in the hot, and then I'll pump a bucket of cold to add so it won't scald you to ashes," said Zillia.

"All right." Patsy stared down at the floor and chewed the end of her braid.

"We're going to take care of you, don't worry." Zillia patted her shoulder.

"It's not that. I was just thinking about Jimmy. I'm not sure if I want him going up to glory. It was kinda nice to think of him close by, even if he was in the church yard. 'Course, he's in San Marcus and I'm all the way here now."

Zillia stroked the little girl's smudged cheek. "My parents are up in Heaven, too," she said softly. "But I like to think there's a way for them to know what I'm up to. And sometimes, when I say my prayers, I ask God to give them messages."

Patsy's eyes widened. "Do you think God could give Jimmy a message for me?"

"You can always ask," said Zillia. "I just bet He would."

6

REFUGE

The skin on Soonie's hands burned, and she set the travois down and examined them. Three fresh blisters. No, four, if you counted the one by her thumb. *I can't do this much longer. It's still half a mile to the bridge, perhaps further since we are skirting away from the main road.* She sat down beside the travois and held her canteen to Lone Warrior's cracked lips. "You need more of this."

He swallowed once and lay back. "Soonie, you are a good, tough woman. But we both know this isn't going to work. Just leave me here and get help. I'll be fine." Fresh red flowed through the makeshift bandage on his shoulder.

Soonie closed her eyes. *Lord, I can't leave him here. But I know he's right. I won't be able to go on much longer. Please give me wisdom.*

Looking up, she noticed a solid sheet of color through the ripples of forest trees and dead brown leaves. *A wall. Maybe a house.* Fear gripped her and she fumbled for the travois. *What if evil people live here as well?*

Hesitating, she studied the path. Bushes and briars grew out over the trail, and in some places she'd had to push past saplings the width of her thumb. *Surely someone would have cleared this trail better if they came here recently.*

"Wait here for a moment. I'm going to check something." She tucked her underskirt a little tighter around her husband's shoulders.

He closed his eyes. "I'm not going anywhere," he murmured.

Soonie struggled through the bushes until she reached the battered wooden house. The single, cracked window visible to her was too dirty to see through. She tiptoed to a sagging front porch, listening at every step, but the property was quiet as a church on Saturday. No animal sounds came from the broken down shed a bit further on.

A weather-warped door hung from one hinge. After a brief struggle, she pushed it open.

Dust filled her senses as soon as she stepped inside the cabin, along with the pungent odor of must and mouse droppings. She held her sleeve over her nose and mouth. The room felt barren, like it hadn't held a human spirit for many years. In the dim light trickling in from the windows, Soonie made out a brick hearth, a table with two rickety chairs, and a bed with a rotted straw tick. Mice scampered past her feet when she stepped forward, and the floor protested beneath her feet. In this desperate moment, the place seemed like a grand cathedral of refuge.

How in the world am I going to get him in here? She went back out to the ancient porch, which seemed as though it could collapse with every step. *I can't leave him by himself for too long . . . it's getting colder, and he needs shelter and rest.*

In front of the house sat the remains of a chicken coop. Rusted wire sagged to the ground, and rotted boards stuck up in the air like broken bones. Soonie picked her way through the brush and thorn bushes in the yard and pulled on a couple of the boards. Most were useless, but the termites had spared a few. She dragged these to the porch and laid them across the steps. Pushing against this makeshift ramp, she tested them with her full weight to make sure they would hold. *This will work. This has to work.*

Lone Warrior lay where she'd left him, his eyes closed. His chest rose and fell unevenly.

"My love, I have somewhere for you to stay. I just have to get you there." She touched his face, her fingers light brown against his dark skin.

He opened his eyes slowly, as though the effort pained him. His mouth turned up in a weak smile. "All right."

Pain shot through her fingers as she lifted the travois once more, but she gritted her teeth and moved forward. *A little further. Just a little further. I can do this. I can do all things through Christ who strengthens me.*

Once she reached the ramp, she stopped and checked to make sure he was still tied on to the travois. "Don't want you slipping off," she said.

Lone Warrior gazed up at the porch roof with wide eyes. "Who owns this place?"

"I don't know, but I'm going to try to start a fire in the stove and boil some water. I have to at least clean your wound. I need to redress it . . . maybe find something for us to eat. Hold tight, this is going to be a little bit bumpy."

"All right." Lone Warrior took a deep breath and closed his eyes.

"I love you so much. I hate to see you in pain." A tear slipped down Soonie's face and she bent to kiss her husband's cheek.

"Hey, none of that." Lone Warrior wiped the tear with his thumb. "You need to be strong for both of us. Get me into that house and we'll rest. Maybe you can go for help a little later this afternoon."

'Maybe." She swallowed the rest of her tears and picked up the travois once more.

Pulling with all her strength, she managed to drag the craft up the ramp and into the house. She placed it down with care, but the action still caused a cloud of dust to rise up around them.

Lone Warrior coughed.

"Sorry. I know it's not the best place, but it's better than being out in the open. Let's get you off those sticks." She considered moving him to the bed, but she wasn't sure she could lift him up there, and anyway, the straw tic was disgusting. She sighed. The whole cabin was filthy, but it was still shelter from the weather, and protection from wild beasts if and when she went for help.

She spread her underskirt over the worst of the grime and helped her husband roll onto the material. Rolling up his jacket, she tucked it under his head. After cutting the shawl free, she covered him over once again. "There you are. Snug as a baby in a sling. I have to figure out how to get a fire started."

"Clean the chimney first," Lone Warrior murmured.

"Right." Soonie found an old broom in the corner and poked it up the fireplace. A shower of leaves, ashes and bird nests came down into the grate. She swept them out and to the side and kept poking until nothing else came down. "I think that's done it."

The mantel was a thin frame that stuck out from the wall a few inches. When she ran her hand along the top, her fingers closed around a flint box. "Wonderful." She showed it to Lone Warrior. "I'll fetch some wood and be right back."

"And I will be here."

Wisps of grey cloud had crept over the blue while she brought the travois inside, and a new chill filled the air. Soonie shivered as she searched the cabin yard for dry wood. There was plenty now, but the air felt heavy and thick. *Looks like we're in for a storm. I'd better gather extra.*

Flashes of lightning jabbed the sky. She brought in several armloads of wood, stacking it by the wall closest to the fireplace.

On the fourth load, thick drops of rain began to dot the ground. Her heart sank. *I can't go for help in the heavy rain. Perhaps it will let up soon.*

She rushed the last armload of wood inside, built a fire, and used a bit of hay from the old mattress as kindling. In a few moments, a cheerful little flame crackled in the grate.

"The fire feels nice," Lone Warrior murmured.

A rusted bucket stood in the corner, and Soonie dumped the dust and grime out on the porch and went into the rain to fill it in the creek she'd noticed earlier. When she got back inside, she hung it over the fire. "Hopefully it will hold enough to boil the water." She glanced over at Lone Warrior. His eyes were closed, and his chest rose and fell in a deep rhythm. His skin was still clammy but looked better than it had out in woods.

She felt his forehead. No fever. But when she pulled back the bandage to check his shoulder, the jagged wound was red and angry, though the bleeding had finally stopped.

For a few moments, she knelt over him and prayed. Then, with tears on her eyelashes, she went back to work.

As the rain stopped, darkness closed around the cabin like a glove covering a fist. Soonie boiled a handful of her jerky in some water and fed the broth to Lone Warrior a bit at a time.

His swallows came with difficulty, and every few sips he rested his head back as though the effort was almost too much.

Soonie smoothed the creases in his forehead. "Remember that time we heard the wolves?" she murmured.

"Yes." Lone Warrior's lips turned up at the corners. "The moon was so full that night. I thought it might fall out of the sky and roll along the plains."

"*I* thought we'd be eaten by the wolves," Soonie spooned another bite of broth from the bowl. "Our fire was so tiny, with no wood to build it up. Those shaggy beasts surrounding us." She pressed her hand to her heart. "I've only been that frightened a few times in my life."

"What were the other times?" Lone Warrior rolled over to face her.

"That time on the hillside, when I thought Hal's men were going to kill me and Molly." *And right now.*

"We danced," Lone Warrior said. "We danced in the moonlight and yelled and sang. Those wolves didn't know what to make of us."

Closing her eyes, Soonie remembered the wildness of the night. The scent of sweat and tears, tears of laughter at the absurdity of their dance. The howling of the wolves and the sounds their moccasins made as they slapped the sand in rhythm. The joyous bubble of relief that swelled in her heart as one by one, the wolves skulked away. *We survived then. We will make it through this, too. Both of us.*

After Lone Warrior finished eating, he fell into a fitful sleep. Soonie watched him as his head jerked and his mouth quivered. *Lord, give him peace in his sleep.*

She finished off the broth and curled up next to him on the bare, dirty floor. *I might as well get some rest. No one is going to find us in the dark.*

7

LONG NIGHT

Wylder's piebald mare neighed. She picked up her hooves with care, shaking mud off at each step.

"Sorry, girl." Wylder patted her neck. "I know this isn't the best night to be out, but at least the rain's lightened."

A deluge had begun right as the party crossed the iron bridge and continued for the next three hours.

Instead of turning back, they pushed on to Del Valle, where they started a fire in a little pit under the porch of the tiny whitewashed building that served for the post office. They rubbed their hands over the puny flame, shivering. The sheriff and Grandpa lit pipes. Thin streams of smoke floated out and fizzled in the rain.

"We'll hit Austin in a few hours. Do ya know the name of the fellow they were supposed to borrow the horses from?" The sheriff pulled off his worn leather vest, shook off the water droplets, then hung it by the fire where they'd put their overcoats and jackets.

Grandpa pulled out a creased letter from his pocket and studied it. "Good thing I kept this paper dry. Just so happens they did mention the business. Mr. Bollen's Livery."

"That's mighty fortunate," said the sheriff. "Maybe if we can find Mr. Bollen, he can tell us exactly when they left . . . or if they even showed up for the horses at all."

Wylder pulled hunks of corn bread from a basket and passed them around. "They must have been delayed somehow, and then when this rain came, found some place to shelter until it passed, like we're doing."

Sheriff removed his pipe long enough to take a bite of bread, yellow crumbs sticking to his walrus mustache. "Walt, your granddaughter's a sweet young lady. But you know how folks in these parts act when they see Indians. In my view, an Indian can be good or bad, same as any other man. But that's not the way some people see it, especially those who fought in the wars and such."

Doesn't he realize we already know that? Wylder picked up a stick and began to scrape the mud off his boots, though the effort was fruitless since they'd be right back out in the muck in a few moments. He favored his father's Swedish blood, so when alone he rarely experienced the stares and snickers reserved for people of native heritage. But he still remembered when he was a little boy.

His mother would wear her deerskins into town, her head held high. By then they'd lived in Bastrop for years and most of the business owners knew and trusted their family, but he'd never forgotten the one day she'd stepped into a new business and been asked to leave by the proprietor. Even as a little boy, his hands balled into fists and he'd charged the shopkeeper.

His mother pulled him back and pushed him out the door. "No, my little one," she'd said, her dark hair whipping around her face. "We do not follow hate with hate. God must show that man the truth. We will go to a different store."

Though Wylder obeyed his mother, the incident changed his life forever. He'd decided if he wasn't allowed to defend his culture, he didn't want anyone to know about it. When possible, he avoided going into town with his mother, though he knew this hurt her. If she presented him with any small token of his Comanche heritage, he'd hide it in his room. He refused to wear clothing suggestive of his culture.

Soonie had been different. She'd begged her mother for stories of their ancestors and asked to hear Comanche chants and songs over and over again. She wore native clothing any time she was allowed; letting her hair flow long and free when the other girls wore bonnets.

An unspoken respect had always been between them, an acceptance of the sides they had chosen. But this time, after they found his sister and brought her home to safety, Wylder would find it hard to stay quiet. *Especially when this young man has led her into such danger.* His grip tightened around the stick. He walked to the edge of the porch and flung it into the rain.

"Well." Grandpa stood and scratched his belly. "Looks like it's letting up a bit. Better get going if we're gonna make it to Austin by nightfall."

Wylder glanced at the Sheriff, then back to Grandpa. "Y'all don't think we'll find them this afternoon, do you?"

The sheriff shrugged his broad shoulders. "I don't know. I have this hunch they got stuck in Austin somehow."

Grandpa Walt laid a hand on his arm. "Don't worry, boy. We're gonna find Soonie. Until then, we must place her in the hands of the Almighty."

"Daisy, Daisy, give me your answer, do."

Patsy's childish voice was sweet and high as she rocked Margo's cradle. Firelight gleamed on the little girl's russet hair, now washed and plaited into two braids, just as Zillia used to wear her hair when she was a child.

The rain stopped, with supper dishes washed and dried an hour ago. Orrie had fallen asleep listening to a wild story about gunslingers from Patsy, who seemed to have no end of tales in her head. She'd said she always told stories to her brothers and sisters.

Zillia was thankful for the little girl's presence. She was helpful and respectful, and a welcome distraction while they waited for news from the search party.

I'm sure they'll find them. Probably some misunderstanding. Old Mr. Miller at the Post Office doesn't always interpret those telegrams right. No one had considered the possibility that Soonie and her husband wouldn't be found by nightfall. The sudden storm was sure to have thrown them for a loop. *They'll most likely find each other and all stay in Del Valle for the night. Or they might have gotten as far as Austin. They wouldn't be able to travel all the way to the city and back.*

"Oh!" She covered her face with her hands and took a deep breath.

"Are you all right, Mrs. Eckhart? Baby Margo is asleep." Patsy stared up at her, frowning.

Zillia tried to smile. "I'm trying not to worry about my friend, Soonie, the girl Mr. Eckhart went to find."

"Yep." Patsy sat down in the chair again and put her chin in her hands. "I'm wondering how my mamma is. And little Pearl. And my big brother, Wade. And baby Ida."

A twinge of guilt crept over Zillia. She went over to the chair and put her arm around the little girl. "I'm sure your mamma will be back for you. And she'll bring your brother and sisters, too."

"No she won't." Patsy stuck out her chin. "She left Wade and Pearl with Aunt Freda in Smithville. She left 'em in the night so Aunt Freda wouldn't know to stop her. Then she brought me to

Granny's 'cause Granny said she'd take me off her hands if I earned my keep. Ma took the baby and runned off with a man. Said they were going to San Antone and they weren't ever coming back." Tears ran down her cheeks, and her lip began to tremble. She hid her face in Zillia's shoulder and sobbed.

"Oh, poor, poor dear." Zillia held her tight and stroked her hair for several minutes, until she was able to calm down. "You've been so brave and good. I'm sorry you had to go through this."

"I tried to help Granny," Patsy said through her tears. "But I couldn't make her better. What will I do in this world if she dies?"

"Don't you worry about that," Zillia said, lifting her chin. "We'll figure something out."

Patsy wiped her tears with the corner of Zillia's old apron she'd been lent to help with the dishes. "Do you promise?"

"Of course I promise. But now I think it's time for you to go to bed."

The little girl went through the side door to Soonie's tiny old room, and Zillia followed with a lantern. Earlier in the day she'd dusted the shelves and put fresh sheets on the straw tic. There hadn't been time to change out the straw, but it seemed clean enough, and the house cats did a good job keeping mice out. Strings of feathers and bright leaves covered the walls from collections Soonie had put together when she was a child. Zillia had found a cheery quilt to spread over the bed, and some of Soonie's keepsakes, including a rag doll, made the room more appealing to girlish eyes.

Patsy turned with a bright smile. "I get to sleep here all by myself? I don't have to share the bed with anyone?"

"You can have it all to yourself. You won't be lonely, will you?"

Patsy picked up the doll and stroked the calico dress. "Can I sleep with this dolly?"

"Sure you can. Soonie wouldn't mind."

"All right, then, I think I'll be fine."

Zillia tucked Patsy into bed and said a prayer over her. She picked up the lantern. "Sleep well. Maybe we'll find out some good news about your grandma tomorrow."

The little girl smiled a sleepy smile. "And I bet Mr. Eckhart will find your friend."

As Zillia went back to the kitchen, a new resolution settled into her heart. *I will help this little girl. I will make sure she has a better life waiting in the future.*

Sleep was hard to find without Wylder next to her, and Zillia spent most of the night reading her Bible by candlelight or pacing her room, with no companion but her own long shadows. She checked Orrie once, in his little bedroom. Margo slept peacefully no matter which of the squeaky boards Zillia trod on by mistake.

Why didn't they come home tonight? Did they at least make it to Austin? I hope they were all right in the storm. Oh, Soonie . . . She sank down on the bed and buried her head in the feather pillow.

8

HEALING PLANT

In the morning, Soonie woke with a start and clutched at the small of her back. She groaned. Though she'd spent months sleeping on the ground in the wilderness she'd never enjoyed the experience. The bed in their tipi was stacked with comfortable blankets and furs, like a cozy nest.

She hobbled to the fireplace and stoked up the fire. As she watched the sparks fling against the chimney stones, a decision formed itself in her mind.

I must go for help somehow. I will have to leave Lone Warrior here and trust God to care for him. He needs medicine, warmth, and better food.

She stroked her husband's chiseled face, usually strong and determined, now pale and drawn with pain. *Why, why did I ask for us to come? How can I still deny the possibility of evil when it's stared me in the face so many times?*

Lone Warrior's eyes fluttered open. "Oh, there you are."

"Where else would I be?" Soonie attempted to smile. "I need to fetch more water. I'll be back in a few minutes."

Giving a hint of a nod, he closed his eyes again.

Dawn had come. Blood-red clouds swarmed the sky, little pools of yellow peering down at her like accusing eyes. Water still dripped from sodden branches, and sparrows fluffed dowdy feathers on the rotted fence posts.

Soonie rushed down to the little stream and filled the bucket and her canteen. "God, give me wisdom!" she cried out, since Lone Warrior couldn't hear her now. "I can't lose him. I can't! Please!" She sank down to her knees on a rock beside the stream, sobs filling her lungs and taking every bit of air.

"Trust me, Soonie. Trust me."

She opened her eyes and looked up. God had spoken to her many times; she knew His voice well. "God, I don't know what to do. Please show me something–something to give me hope."

A flash of white a few yards away caught her eye. At first her mind dismissed it as a scrap of paper or a leftover bright fall leaf. A flower would be impossible this time of year. And yet . . . *Could it be?* A cluster of tiny flowers, with delicate, fern-like leaves.

"Yarrow," she whispered. "Is it really a yarrow?"

With shaking hands, she plucked several stems from the plant. She bundled the fuzzy, spicy-scented leaves, picked up the water and hurried back into the cabin.

Lone Warrior smiled when she came in. "You are so beautiful," he said.

"I'm filthy." She pulled the packet from where she'd tucked it into her dress. "But wait until you see what I found."

"Something to eat?" His voice was hopeful.

"Better."

He pushed himself up on his good elbow. "How could anything be better than food?"

"Lone Warrior, you lay back down this instant!" She scolded. "Do you want to start bleeding again?"

An old skillet, scavenged from the cupboard, served to crush the leaves to a pulp. Soonie pulled back the bandage on Lone Warrior's shoulder.

'This is going to hurt," she told him. "But it will help."

"What you got there?" His eyes rolled towards the crushed leaves.

"Yarrow. I've seen Molly use it in her clinic for small wounds and cuts. It should help draw out the poisons the bullet might have put in your blood. It will help the blisters on my hands too. And you can drink some in a tincture to help with pain and fever." She pursed her lips. "I've seen flowers in the fall, but never this late in the winter. God must have sent this little plant just for us."

A ghost of a smile appeared on Lone Warrior's lips, but turned to a grimace when she pressed the poultice against the wound.

"Sorry." She wrapped the bandage tightly around the mashed-up leaves. "We'll leave the yarrow until I return. Let me just get this tincture prepared, and then I can go."

Lone Warrior patted her arm with his good hand. "My Soonie-girl. You are wonderful."

"I will be more wonderful if I can get you some help."

He rolled to his side and pushed himself up on his good elbow, grimacing. "The night's sleep was good for me, I think. I'm a little better today. Go and do not worry for me."

Soonie gave him a slanted look. "All right, but I'd better not find you chopping wood when I come back."

More water was soon boiled and cooled, and the tincture prepared. Soonie surveyed the cabin. There was nothing else to do but to leave the love of her life behind. *If someone else finds him–*

This could be the last time I see him alive. Tears fell thick and fast, and she could not stop them as she bent to kiss his lips. "My love, I have to go now. It shouldn't take longer than a few hours to get help and come back for you."

He lifted his left hand and stroked her cheek. "Don't worry. I'll be here when you return. I'll be fine."

As she stepped out the door, she heard his voice, low at first, then rising through the cabin walls. He was singing in Kiowa, the song of a warrior who has come home in triumph.

###

The stable hadn't been opened when the search party reached town for the night, so Wylder, his grandpa and the sheriff sheltered at a small boarding house. They arrived at the livery stable just as Mr. Bollen stepped outside to turn the open sign around.

Grandpa explained the situation. "Have you seen my granddaughter?"

Mr. Bollen ran his hand along his chin. "Yep, boys, one of the sheriff's men brought two horses back to me yesterday afternoon. Said someone had turned 'em in as stolen property and they recognized my double R brand. I said they wasn't stolen, at least when I sent 'em out." He leaned over the fence and squinted at Grandpa Walt. "I rented 'em to your granddaughter and her husband yesterday morning at eight of the clock. The Injun man had a letter from my good friend, Captain Wilkenson, and I trust whatever he tells me." He stepped back. "Besides, I liked the look of him. Seemed like a good man, fer an Injun."

"And the men that turned them in to the sheriff didn't give any details?" asked the sheriff.

"Nope. The deputy didn't even know who'd brought 'em in. The whole thing seemed fishy to me. But the horses still had packs tied to the saddles, and once I explained things to the deputy he turned 'em over to me so I could give them back to their rightful owners, if they came back. Hang on a minute." Mr. Bollen disappeared into the stable.

"What are you thinking, Sheriff?" said Grandpa.

The sheriff pulled off his hat and ran his fingers through his dusty blond hair. "To tell the truth, I'm a bit flummoxed. Either the horses were stolen from Soonie and her husband, and then recovered by good folk who wanted to make sure they were returned, or something very wrong happened out on the trail. I'm thinking Soonie must not have gotten too far, or the folks who found these horses would have turned them in at the jailhouse, not rustled them all the way back to Austin."

Mr. Bollen came back outside, carrying two large saddlebags. "That's the thing. Deputy said they were left at the post office in Del Valle around five of the clock yesterday. He happened to be passing through."

"We just missed him," the sheriff mumbled.

Wylder unfastened one of the bags and looked inside. Beaded clothing, small bundles wrapped in brown paper. There it was. He pulled out the leather-covered book. "This is the Bible we gave my sister before she left for her teaching position." His fingers shook. It was one thing to hear the stable owner's story, but this was tangible proof he couldn't deny. Soonie had been here, at this very place. And now his sister was gone.

When Uncle Isak had asked Soonie to journey to North Texas as a teacher, she'd acted so excited, so certain God had called her to the task. He'd begged her not to go, but she'd been so happy. After a time, he'd given up and tried to share in her joy. He stuffed the Bible back into the bag. *Why didn't I put my foot down? Why didn't I try harder to make her stay? Not that she'd ever listened to me before.*

"She's so stubborn," he said aloud before he'd realized.

"Yes, she is." Grandpa Walt took the bags and loaded them on his horse. "But it's held her in good stead all these years, and she'll fight through whatever she must to come out ahead once more." He turned to Mr. Bollen and shook his hand. "Thank you kindly for the information. Looks like we have more searching to do."

9

DESPERATE FRIEND

Zillia stirred a large pot of oatmeal, fighting the urge to look out the kitchen window to the front road every few minutes. *Watching's not going to bring them back faster.*

Margo banged her spoon on the table, baby gurgles turning into impatient cries.

"Silly girl." Zillia crumbled a bit of Johnny cake on the plate in front of her. "I'm not going to let you starve."

Patsy emerged from the tiny side room with a giant borrowed apron tied around her waist and her hair already braided in one braid, pulled around the side.

Zillia smiled. *Mama taught me how to braid my hair like that when I was little.* "Did you sleep well, Patsy?"

"I sure did. It was nice not to have fleas in the bed, or Pearl waking me up. She doesn't mean to, but she kicks in her sleep." The little girl looked around. "Can I help with something?"

"Sure, thank you. Can you tell Orrie it's time for breakfast? I want to get all the chores done in haste since we need to be in town by ten o'clock this morning. Our church is doing a Christmas play, and today is the last practice. Can you believe Friday is Christmas? Only two days away!"

"Aw, Christmas," Patsy yawned and rubbed her eyes. "We never had Christmas. 'Cept sometimes Ma bought an orange for us all to share." She frowned. "I think once."

Zillia's spoon froze over the oatmeal pot. *Never had Christmas?* Even in the hardest years, when it was just her and Orrie, Grandpa Walt and Grandma Louise had always opened their home and shared the tree, holiday treats, and lights. She couldn't fathom Christmas being considered a normal day.

"This year, Patsy, you shall have a Christmas," she promised.

Patsy looked down at the floor. "It sounds nice. But what about Wade and little Pearl?"

Zillia put down the spoon and sank down to one knee to look the little girl in the eye. "We don't know where to find your aunt right now. Do you know how to get to her house?"

Patsy shook her head, and a tear dripped down to her chin. "It was in the night, and we only went there once."

Zillia handed her a handkerchief. "Your Granny can probably tell us where to find them, but we have to wait until she gets better. So it might be after December 25th. But I promise they will have a Christmas too, even if it's a little bit late. All right?"

Patsy nodded and wiped her eyes. "Sounds good to me."

"It's going to be lovely, don't you worry," said Zillia. "Now go wake up Orrie."

Zillia was tempted to stop by the Eckharts' farm before she headed to town, but by the time she had everyone dressed and the chores finished it was too late. *Grandma Louise would have sent word if there was any news from Wylder.* She loaded the three children in the wagon. It was nice to have Patsy along to make sure Margo stayed still on the trip. Orrie would have tried his best, but she didn't think he was quite old enough to hold the baby the whole way. Usually Wylder or Grandma Louise came along on such trips.

I'll stop at the post office after the practice to see if they've received another telegraph.

All the children were lined up on the church steps waiting for them, along with Mrs. Fowler.

"Good morning, Zillia." Mrs. Fowler adjusted her straw bonnet, which was piled high with fake cherries and blossoms. She held the church door open for the children to troop inside. "And Patsy, how are you today? Did you sleep well?"

"Yes, Ma'am." Patsy gave her a shy smile. "How is Granny?"

"I went by to see her this morning. She was sleeping."

Patsy clasped her thin fingers together and rested her chin on them. "She sleeps all the time. I hope she gets better soon."

Zillia caught Mrs. Fowler's eye. The preacher's wife frowned and gave a slight shake of her head. "I'm going outside, Zillia. I'll be right back."

She must not be doing so well Even if she gets better, Patsy can't possibly go back to that horrible house. "Patsy, would you like to be a part of the play?" Zillia fought to keep the worry from her voice. "We could always use a shepherdess."

"What's a shepherdess?"

Zillia walked over to the pew where all the costumes had been laid out in preparation for the day. Children milled around, pulling out muslin wings and halos made from beaten tin.

"A shepherdess is a girl shepherd. The shepherds must have been very special to God, because he sent an angel to them to tell about the Christ child's birth before anyone else."

"Oh yes, I remember this story. Sometimes our neighbor took us to church." Patsy eyed the row of costumes. "What do they wear?"

"Here's a robe." Zillia handed Patsy a burlap garment with ragged holes for the sleeves. "You fasten it around your waist with a sash, like this." She turned the little girl around and tied a bow. "There."

Patsy smoothed the burlap and nodded. "I'll be the best shepherdess I can be."

"I'm sure you will," said Zillia.

"You can come with me, Patsy," Orrie said with a grin. "I know all about being a shepherd."

"But do you know how to be a shepherd*ess*?" Patsy squinted at him.

"Come on." Orrie started towards the stage, and she trotted after him, the burlap rustling as she moved.

"Mrs. Eckhart, I need help again." Katie came forward and turned to the side, displaying a jagged tear in her Mary robe.

"Oh goodness. Hang on, I'll try to find a sewing kit."

Colored light washed over the pews from the ornate stained-glass windows. Zillia began to rummage through the piles of props and materials arranged on the front pew.

Mrs. Fowler came through the front door and down the center aisle. "I'll take care of that." She put a hand on Zillia's shoulder. Her face was drawn and white, though a hint of a smile quirked in the corner of her mouth. "Zillia, hurry outside, dear," she said in a low voice. "Someone to see you."

Zillia's heart fell to the bottom of her stomach. In the hustle and bustle of preparing for rehearsal, she'd managed to forget about her missing friend for a short while. She picked up Margo, who had been playing with scraps of fabric, and rushed outside.

"Zillia, thank goodness!" Soonie stood at the door. Her hair swung above her shoulders, and strands were plastered to her forehead. Her cheap calico dress was torn to tatters. Despite these factors, her delicate features and dark brown eyes conveyed a beauty that couldn't be hidden by such trifles.

Zillia stepped back and surveyed her friend. "You're all muddy, and where is your shawl? It's too cold to be out dressed like this." She peered over her friend's shoulder. "And where is your husband?"

Tears flowed down Soonie's face. "Oh, Zillia, he was shot by some terrible men for no reason. They took our horses and left him to bleed to death. I had to leave him behind and come for help. He's not as bad as he was yesterday but I still couldn't let him walk that far."

"Soonie, how terrible! Of course we'll come." Zillia paused. "But Wylder went after you yesterday. I wonder why he didn't find you?"

"We had to get away from the road. I left him a sign, but he must not have seen it because of the rain."

Mrs. Fowler stepped out from the doorway where she'd been listening. "Zillia, Pastor Fowler is right next door in the church study. If you will go tell him the situation, I'm sure he can take our buggy and a few other men to help. The buggy will get there faster than a heavy wagon, especially with the road still muddy in places. And Soonie, of course you'll have to go so they can find where your husband is staying."

Zillia handed Margo to Mrs. Fowler. "Would you be willing to care for the children so I can go too?"

"Of course. We'll finish up with rehearsal and I'll take them to my house. They can play with my children." Mrs. Fowler patted

Soonie's hand. "Don't worry. God is with your husband right now. All will be well."

Soonie wiped her tears and nodded. "We need to hurry," she said in a wispy voice.

Zillia moved towards the study and Soonie followed with wavering steps. Zillia turned and studied her face. "Have you had anything to eat?"

"Not much," her friend replied. "I'm fine."

"No you're not." Zillia went over to the buckboard and rummaged around in the back until she found the lunch pail. Pulling out a hunk of Johnny cake and a piece of salt pork, she handed them to Soonie. "Here, we brought plenty. Sit down and eat this while I go talk to Pastor Fowler."

Her friend nodded and sank back down on the porch. "We need to take something for Lone Warrior too."

"All right, there's plenty in this lunch pail. I'm sure Mrs. Fowler can find something for the children. I'll be right back."

Pastor Fowler didn't answer when she rapped on the study door, so she pushed it open. Two feet cased in worn leather shoes were propped up on the desk, and gentle snores came from under a newspaper.

Zillia tapped the man on his shoulder. "Pastor, please wake up, we need you."

The newspaper rustled, and Pastor Fowler pulled it from his face with thin fingers. "Zillia, hello." His feet thudded on the floor.

"Sorry about that, my daughter's new baby is keeping us up at all hours." He chuckled. "Cute little rascal."

His eyebrows drew down over his beak-like nose as Zillia explained about Soonie and Lone Warrior. He jumped to his feet and pulled on a tweed jacket, which had been draped over a chair. "We have some old blankets in the poor barrel. Let's gather those and see if we can find the doctor. If he's not there, we'll try to get a few other men to follow on horseback. The buggy only seats five, three if someone has to lie down in the back."

"And we must send someone to tell Grandma Louise. She's been worried sick."

Pastor Fowler's forehead creased. "I'll send my grandson. He's thirteen and can ride like the wind. He knows where the Eckharts live."

Zillia ran back out to Soonie. "Come on, we'll get the buggy hitched up, and Mr. Fowler's going over to the clinic to find the doctor."

Hope sprang into Soonie's eyes. "We have a clinic here now?"

"Yes, when old Doctor Peterson retired last year, we got a younger doctor from Pennsylvania. He tore down the old office and built a new clinic. He stitched up Wylder last year when he cut his hand on a fence."

Soonie closed her eyes. "Wylder . . . I wish he was here. Hopefully he will find us."

10

REUNION

Wylder pulled his coat closer and rubbed his hands together before gathering the reins again. Each breath sent a small cloud into the air. The rain had passed; thank goodness for that, but a thick fog wafted through the trees like clumps of cotton.

"It's going to be tough to search for anything in this," said the sheriff.

Grandpa Walt took a swig from his canteen. "Yup. But we know God Almighty loves Soonie more than Wylder and I do. He's got her in His hands, and He will lead us to her. I feel, right here," he thumped his chest with a gloved hand, "That we'll find her today. I just feel it."

"I hope you're right," murmured Wylder. *And I hope she's safe.* He wouldn't even allow himself to think the words "not dead."

They passed through Del Valle, scouring the sides of the road and knocking on the doors of the few homes they encountered.

One door was answered by a burly man who wore nothing but long john underwear. "Howdy?"

"Hello." Wylder held out a family photograph taken when Soonie was thirteen, the one where she'd insisted, as usual, on wearing her buckskin skirt. "Have you seen this girl? She's older now, and she was traveling with her husband."

The man squinted at the photograph. "Looks like an Injun to me. What'd she do? She wanted by the law?" He nodded over Wylder's shoulder at the sheriff.

Wylder worked to steady his breathing. *I will not hurt this man over words. It's not worth it.*

The sheriff cleared his throat. "No sir, the woman in the picture is a beloved family member of these folks, and we believe she's in danger. We're trying to find her."

The man spat on the ground. "One less Injun makes the world a better place, if ya ask me. Now if that's all you're after, I'm going back to bed. This weather's foul."

He slammed the door in their faces.

A muscle twitched in the sheriff's cheek. "So much hate in folks' hearts."

"He doesn't even know Soonie. Doesn't know the good she's done or the love she has for people." Wylder shook his head. "Makes no sense."

"We should have sent someone to fetch them from Austin," said Grandpa Walt. "But your Uncle Isak always came by himself, and he never mentioned any dangerous encounters."

"Maybe he didn't want to worry us," said Wylder.

The party of three rode on in silence for several miles, with only the calls of the cardinals to keep up their spirits. The fog lifted in bits, and they were soon able to carry on their search in better visibility.

But we might have already missed them. Wylder tried to keep his hands from trembling. He ached to reach out, to tear something to pieces. The closer they came to Bastrop, the more this anger built in his heart. Finally, he halted. "Grandpa, I have to stop for a moment. I'll catch up to you."

Grandpa Walt's eyebrows drew together. He sighed. "I understand, Boy. Go on, then. Sheriff n' I will wait here."

Wylder tied his horse to a bush and stomped off a few yards down the road. He'd battled with his anger since he was a little boy and always found chopping wood as a healthy way to let it out. *Don't have a woodpile or an axe.* He picked up a good-sized limb and smashed it into a tree, over and over again, until it was splintered and scattered on the forest floor. He threw down the remains of the branch and picked up another. The movements felt good, and his rage dwindled down into a smoldering flame.

As he reached for his fourth limb, he saw it, a flicker of color, fluttering at the very edge of his vision. He blinked. *There it was again.* He took a few steps, hardly daring to breath. A tattered ribbon of blue, his sister's favorite color. Above, a crude carving of a bird, beak stretched and pointing north.

"Grandpa!" he yelled. "Sheriff! I found something!"

The buggy jostled through the mud, making Soonie's headache. She tried resting it against the wall, but it only felt worse.

Zillia leaned over and peered into her face. "Are you all right? Poor dear. As soon as we get home, I'll fix you a hot supper."

Soonie gave a tiny smile. "I'd rather have a bath first." A pang of guilt stabbed her heart. *I can't believe I'm thinking such a thing, with Lone Warrior hungry and waiting for me.* She closed her eyes. *Soon it will be all over, and he'll be with the doctor. And this time, we have people to help us. I'm so close.*

Zillia squeezed her hand. "Don't worry, everything is going to be fine."

Mr. Rawlings, a blacksmith, had agreed to come. He sat by Pastor Fowler in the driving seat of the buggy.

Soonie peered out the window, and then rapped on the dividing wall. The carriage came to a halt and Pastor Fowler came around to the door. "Yes?"

"I left the mark on the tree right around here." Soonie stumbled out of the carriage and glanced through the oaks, cedars and elms that lined the road. "Yes, I remember this twisted cedar tree. Here it is." She pointed to the tattered ribbon. "We need to go this way. There's a bit of a road."

Pastor Fowler frowned. "I'm not sure if the buggy will make it all the way through. We'll try to get as far as possible."

Soonie swiveled to face the pastor "The cabin's close. It won't be a long way to carry him, if we have to. I made a travois."

"You did?" A new respect crept into Mr. Rawlings voice.

Soonie nodded and took off in the direction of the bird's beak pointed.

An indention in the soft mud caught her attention. *Fresh hoof prints. Two–three horses heading towards the cabin. Could someone have seen the smoke over the trees? If they hurt him*–She clenched her fists.

"We need to hurry," she called over her shoulder. "It looks like someone's already there!"

"I'm coming," said Pastor Fowler, as he attempted to steer the horses around the worst of the mud puddles. "It's no use. We're going to have to leave the buggy here." He wound the reins around a tree trunk, and then reached out and pulled a shotgun from behind the seat.

Zillia got out of the buggy and put her hand on Soonie's shoulder. "Don't worry. Maybe they came to help."

Soonie couldn't keep the quiver from her voice. "Or it's the owner of the cabin. Or Zillia, what if it's the same men who hurt him in the first place?" She took off in a sprint through the trees. Mud spattered her clothes, and branches tore at her exposed skin. She paid them no heed.

Horses nickered as she entered the clearing. Her heart sank as she saw her own saddlebag draped over the back of a chestnut. Something seemed familiar about the horses, but she took no time to mull over where she'd seen them. She drew her knife from her belt and crept up the steps to the cabin.

Low male voices came from inside. And then a laugh. A laugh! *How dare they?* She held the knife high and swung open the door.

"Soonie, you made it back." Wylder rose and held out his hand. "You can put that down. We're here now."

"Oh." The knife clattered to the floor and she sank against the door. Grandpa Walt and the sheriff chuckled.

Soonie covered her face with her hands and staggered over to Lone Warrior, who sat, cross-legged, by the fire.

He took her hands. "You're trembling. Get closer to the warmth." He kissed her forehead. "I'm glad you made it back. We were about to head to Bastrop."

A spark of anger flared up, overtaking her relief. She sat back and glared at him. "You mean to say they were going to throw you over a saddle and let you ride back to town?"

"That plant must have helped. My shoulder's feeling much better," Lone Warrior protested.

"What if you started bleeding again?" Soonie stood, fighting an urge to stomp her foot. "I've never heard of such a thing. I've brought you a buggy."

Zillia pushed open the door, with Pastor Fowler and Mr. Rawlings right behind her.

Pastor Fowler removed his hat and ran his hand through thinning hair. "Praise the Lord, it's a Christmas miracle!"

Zillia rushed over to Wylder and hugged him. "I missed you," she said. "Don't ever go away again."

"Only if I have to rescue my sister," he promised.

"Zillia, this is Lone Warrior, my husband," Soonie said.

Lone Warrior reached out with one hand, winced, and lowered his arm. "I don't intend to be impolite. It's nice to meet you."

"I'm glad to see you're doing better." Zillia smiled. She looked around the cabin. "I'm sure this is better than the plain ground, but what a dirty place. Let's get you home before the entire house falls down."

Lone Warrior insisted he could walk to the buggy, but Pastor Fowler and the sheriff helped him along.

Soonie gathered the few supplies they had in the cabin and poured the rest of the water on the fire. "Thank you, little cabin," she whispered before she closed the door. "You might be shabby, but you were here at just the right time."

11

AT THE HEARTH

When the buckboard clattered up to Grandma Louise's house, she was standing on the front porch, hair bound up in its usual mound of braids, hand shading weary eyes. She looked older, shrunken into herself.

Soonie popped up over the side of the wagon. She and Lone Warrior had ridden in the back with the children.

As the old woman's eyes fell on her granddaughter, she sagged into a chair on the porch. She brought her apron up to her face, and her shoulders heaved. Soonie ran over to her grandmother. She held her close and stroked the thin gray hair, as though she were the child.

"They said you were all right, but I couldn't believe it until I saw for myself," said the elderly woman in a muffled voice.

Grandpa Walt rode up and gestured over to the scene on the porch. "Guess she's glad."

Zillia hopped down from the wagon to retrieve the children.

Patsy and Orrie were wrapped in blankets in the wagon bed, playing a game of patty-cake.

"Come on children, let's get inside and warm up a bit before we go home." Zillia had given Wylder a few details about Patsy but she hadn't had time to tell the whole story. He'd agreed, in an absent-minded way, to let her stay until Christmas.

Margo was sleeping on Lone Warrior's good shoulder.

He smiled. "She's a sweet little thing. You and Wylder are blessed."

They'd had to stay in town for a while until the doctor finally came back, weary from delivering twins. Though the new doctor didn't know Soonie, he hadn't batted an eye when they'd brought Lone Warrior into the clinic, much to everyone's relief. After cleaning the wound, he'd nodded to Soonie. "The bullet went right through, that's a mercy. But he would have bled out if you hadn't known what to do. Now there isn't much left to fix, it's closed too much for stitching. The wound doesn't seem to be septic." He'd given them a packet of powder, "to dull the pain a bit. But you might just want a bottle of whiskey."

Wylder came around the wagon. "I'll take the baby." He pulled Margo from Lone Warrior's arms. "Might as well come meet Grandma." His voice was gruff.

What's his problem? Can't he just be happy everyone is safe? Zillia rolled her eyes and helped Orrie and Patsy out of the wagon.

After a morning of travel and uncertainty, the warmth of the house felt like arms embracing them. Soonie introduced Lone Warrior to Grandma Louise, Henry and Will.

Grandma Louise wiped her tears and took a few deep breaths. She bustled around, lighting the candles on the Christmas tree and slipping warm cookies and hot drinks into cold hands while everyone told stories of the day.

Finally, she perched on the edge of her seat like a nervous little bird. "I'm thankful to have you home." She folded her hands over her apron, embroidered with traditional red and pink Swedish flowers. "Lone Warrior, you are welcome in this family."

"Thank you." Lone Warrior's eyes traveled around the room. "It's good to be warm and dry.

Soonie gave an account of their adventures. Everyone gasped when she told of the evil men who had shot Lone Warrior.

Grandpa Walt pressed his fingers against his cheeks. "It's a sad story, but it happens more than you think. The sheriff's told me of black folks he's found strung up in trees, and no one knows who put 'em there. A man from an Irish family was beaten for thievery with no proof. No one did anything about it. Even if we found those men, Soonie, and you identified them, they have a fish feather story that would hold up in a court of law. Just 'cause it's the way of things."

Soonie sighed. "I know, Grandpa. It's the world we live in. I think it must make God sad, since He made all of us."

"We've all had our troubles." Grandma Louise traced the embroidery on her apron with a wrinkled finger. "When Walt and I came to this country, we couldn't say more than 'hello' in English. We had some money but were scared to death to spend anything for fear of being robbed. I'll never forget how it felt, standing on the shores of New York with a wagon's worth of belongings and no idea how we'd get to Texas. We might have had white skin, but we had strange clothes and customs, and people treated us like cockroaches."

Zillia sat still, listening to the stories. *And all this time I felt sorry for myself for being poor. I never had anyone throw me out of a place because of poverty. Those men were so evil. We could have been planning a funeral, if it wasn't for Soonie's friend who taught her what to do and God's good mercy.* She glanced over at Wylder. He stared into the fire; his face drawn into a scowl. *I wonder if he realizes how ridiculous he's being.* She put her face in her hands. *He's been patient with me when I made mistakes. I'll just have to wait for him to come around. Hopefully it will be soon.*

Wylder stood and stretched, still not making eye contact with anyone in the room. "It's time we get these children home. What do you think, Zillia?"

Zillia glanced out the window. The sun *was* getting low in the horizon. She squeezed Soonie's hand. "I can hardly bear to leave you, but we'll be back tomorrow."

Soonie nodded. Her eyelids fluttered and she smiled a sleepy smile.

"You must be exhausted," said Zillia. "We'll come in the afternoon. I'm sure Grandma Louise will let you sleep in tomorrow. And what's the day after that?" she asked Orrie, who was curled up next to her feet.

"Christmas!" he shouted.

Christmas in two days. Zillia surveyed the room. *And now everything will be perfect.*

Christmas Eve was spent in a whirlwind of preparation. Patsy helped Zillia in the kitchen and with Margo. Wylder and Orrie brought in load after load of firewood to keep the old stove hot and ready to bake.

"Henry said he'd show me some kitties in the barn today," said Patsy, as she dusted flour over the table. "He said they were just born."

"How sweet," said Zillia a bit absentmindedly. The caramel on the stove was almost thickened, and she had to stir it at just the right speed or it would burn.

"I have a kitty," said Patsy. Her eyes widened. "I have a kitty, and she's at Granny's house. I forgot all about her. Oh Mrs. Eckhart, what if she's frozen to death?" Tears began to stream down the little girl's face.

"Oh, dear." Zillia whisked the caramel off the stove, poured it in a pan, and put the kettle in the washbasin. She wiped Patsy's tears with the corner of her apron. "How big is the kitty? Is it a baby?"

Patsy snuffled. "No, she's a big grown-up cat. She's white and her name is Feather."

"In that case, she'll probably be fine. If she's lived at your granny's this long, she probably hunts mice and has a nice cozy corner of the shed to sleep in."

Patsy's face brightened. "That's true. But what if she's lonely? I bet she misses me."

Zillia patted her shoulder. "How about if we stop by your granny's house tomorrow? The boys can help you look for your kitty. If you find her, you can bring her back here."

"That sounds good," said Patsy slowly. She went over to the washbasin and washed her hands and face.

Children's troubles. Zillia shook her head and smiled. *If only everything could be solved by a kitten, no one would have any problems left to face.*

###

That afternoon, everyone was once again assembled into Grandma Louise's living room.

Grandpa Walt brought down the old Swedish Bible, the fragile pages so thin they were almost translucent. Painstakingly, he translated the Swedish words into the age-old story, the birth of the Christ child, just as he did every Christmas Eve. Other family members owned English Bibles, but the story seemed more special this way.

After a few hours of talking and singing Christmas carols, Zillia noticed Margo's eyes drooping. She went to a back bedroom and sank into the rocking chair with her baby, humming to her the same songs she used to sing to Orrie when he was an infant. The sky glowed red through the window. "Christmas Eve," she sang quietly. "Something's magical about Christmas Eve."

A gentle knock came at the door, and Soonie slipped in. She was back in her buckskins again, and her eyes were much brighter than the day before.

"I hope I'm not disturbing your baby. Just wanted to spend a little time with you."

"Of course not," Zillia said. "I'm glad you came in."

Soonie sat down on the floor, hugging her knees to her chest like she always had when they were little girls. "Can you believe we're so old? And married now?"

Zillia shook her head. "I remember when I used to go to weddings with my parents when I was younger. I always envied the brides in their dresses and veils, with everyone making a fuss over them. I thought it would be forever before it was my turn. And now sometimes it seems like I've been married my whole life." She sighed. "I love your brother, but sometimes he can be so stubborn!"

Soonie played with the fringe on her skirt. "Yes, he's already spoken to me about my 'foolhardy decisions.' One thing I know about Wylder, he only makes a ruckus over someone when he really cares about them. I know if I'm patient, God will show him the truth."

"I know," said Zillia. "Patience is not one of my strengths."

"You had the patience to carry this little one for nine months." Soonie touched Margo's hand.

"She was definitely worth the wait." Zillia gazed down at the perfect eyelashes, settled on chubby cheeks. "Though I'm not ready to have another one for a few years, at least."

Soonie sighed. "We want a baby. But it's hard on the reservation. The others . . . their children run in the dirt. They play with sticks and bits of hide. They don't have much, but even so, their smiles shine like starlight. I go back and forth. But still I hope God will grant our wish."

"Oh Soonie, your baby will have you and Lone Warrior. That will be enough. You'll see."

The door to the bedroom burst open. Margo jumped in Zillia's arms and began to cry.

"Orrie," Zillia hissed. "What on earth? Margo was almost asleep."

Orrie's eyes widened. "Sorry, Zillia, but Wylder told me to tell you. We can't find Patsy. I think she ran away."

12

RESCUE

Zillia carried Margo into the big room. The adults stood in the corner, talking in hushed voices.

Wylder touched her shoulder. "Orrie said they were playing with the kittens in the barn, and Patsy mentioned she needed to go find something. They didn't think anything of it until they realized she'd been gone for a while. When Grandpa came out, he noticed the smallest lantern and a box of matches were missing."

"She might have gone back to your house, Zillia" said Grandma Louise. "It's not far, and if she had the lantern, she could make her way even in the dark."

"Or she could have gone to her granny's." Zillia tapped her chin. "She was telling me about a pet cat there. Maybe she decided to go find it on her own."

"I don't know where Mrs. Barnes lives, so I'll take Will and Henry to look at your house," Grandpa Walt offered.

"I'll take care of Orrie and Margo here. Lone Warrior and Soonie can stay and rest," said Grandma Louise.

Soonie came behind Zillia. "I want to go with them. I've rested plenty." She patted Lone Warrior's hand. "Is that all right with you?"

"Be careful." Lone Warrior took her hand and kissed it.

The corners of Wylder's mouth drew down into a frown. Taking Zillia's hand, he pulled her outside. "Do you think it's safe for him to stay here with Grandma?" he whispered to her.

"Wylder Eckhart! I can't believe you would say such a thing! For one thing, he's wounded. I don't think he's capable of making much trouble. He seems like a good person. Soonie obviously thinks the world of him."

Wylder grunted, turned on his heel, and moved towards the barn with swift strides. "Let's take the horses instead of the wagon," he called over his shoulder. "They'll get us there faster. Since she went on foot, we might even catch her on the road."

Soonie joined Zillia, and they went to the barn to help Wylder. In a short time the horses were saddled and bridled, and they were on their way.

Wylder brought the big lantern, holding it high as they rode. Dim moonlight filtered through the clouds with little effect. But the horses knew the road well, and the mud had dried in most places.

"Oh, I hope we find her." Zillia shivered beneath her shawl. "It's cold out here and she's such a little thing."

"She seems pretty capable, though," said Soonie. "Wylder and I used to camp way out in the woods when we weren't much older."

"What's going to happen to her?" Wylder asked. "I mean, if her grandma doesn't get better?"

"I don't know. Her mother took the baby and ran off with some man. Her brother and sister are staying with her aunt. Mrs. Fowler said it's possible all of the children will have to go to an orphanage in Austin. But that would be just awful," said Zillia. She batted her eyelashes at Wylder.

"I know what that look means." Wylder gave a wry smile. "And I know what you're thinking. We do have room for another, and one extra mouth wouldn't be much. But all three?" He shook his head. "Why don't we wait until after Christmas and see what happens with her granny?"

"If you saw the inside of that house, you wouldn't want to send her back there." Zillia wrinkled her nose. "It was awful."

Soonie drew her horse up closer to Zillia's. "I don't know how people can raise children in places like that," "Even on the reservation where most families have nothing, the women work hard to keep everything sparkling clean. And when someone is sick, all the families pitch in to help."

"That's just it. We offered help several times. The old woman refused it. You saw Patsy, she's just skin and bones. Though I've done my best to fatten her up the last few days."

"She is pretty skinny," Wylder agreed. "We'll see. The most important thing tonight is to bring her back to warmth and light."

A mile from Mrs. Barnes's house, the horses began to nicker and toss their heads. Zillia's mount danced across the road, and she had to dig her heels into the round flanks to get him to settle down.

"Think there's a bear or cougar up ahead?" asked Zillia.

Soonie shook her head. "Probably not in this cold. But something's wrong." She stopped and sniffed the air. "Do you smell that?"

Wylder pulled down his muffler. "Smoke. And more than a campfire. I'd say a building was on fire."

And now they could all see the red glow above the trees.

"It has to be Mrs. Barnes's house," shouted Zillia. "No one else lives out that way." She clicked her tongue and urged her horse forward. Soonie and Wylder's horses thundered behind her.

An orange glow spilled out over the trees, cloaked in thick smoke, like a giant dark beast with a furnace in its belly.

Zillia shouted, "Faster!" to her horse.

"Careful," shouted Wylder, "Milo is high strung!"

The words whipped past her in the night, but she paid them no heed.

When she reached the yard, the air was thick with smoke. Frightened chickens scurried by in the direction of the river. Milo reared back, but she kept her seat and patted his neck.

The entire back end of the dilapidated farmhouse was engulfed in flames. The front door yawned open, orange flickers lighting up the inside.

Zillia dismounted and tied her horse to a fence post, praying it wasn't too rotted to hold the animal. She ran towards the house, cupping her hands around her mouth. "Patsy!" she called. "Are you here?"

"Mrs. Eckhart!" A voice floated down from somewhere high above her. "Mrs. Eckhart? Help! Please!"

Wylder and Soonie's horses reached the yard, and the brother and sister swung down and joined her.

"I hear Patsy, but I can't see her. Wylder, you have to help me!" Zillia shouted above the crackles and screams of the wood.

"Please help me!" The voice was a bit louder now.

"If she can see us, we should be able to see her." Wylder walked closer to the house, scanning the building. "Patsy, where are you? Call out again!"

The limbs of a giant oak several yards from the house rustled, and Patsy's white, tear-streaked face appeared in the farthest reach of the lantern light.

"We're up here."

Sparks and flaming debris fell dangerously close to the branches of the oak. *It could catch fire at any moment.* "Patsy, you have to climb down!" Zillia shouted.

"I can't! I'm too scared."

A ladder leaned against the barn wall, half-covered in bushes. Zillia yanked it up, but the rotted wood splintered in her hands.

"I'm going to search the grounds," Wylder yelled. "Maybe I can find something else to use."

Soonie went to the foot of the tree and stared up at Patsy. "How did you get up there? Did you stand on something?"

Patsy shook her head. The flames leapt higher, and the heat intensified with every moment.

Zillia examined the tree trunk. "I don't know how she did it. The trunk's smooth and there aren't any branches for at least nine feet."

"I could have shimmied up there when I was her age, but now . . ." Soonie shrugged her shoulders.

Wylder lugged over a small barrel and a large cast iron soap pot. "Maybe we can make a stack and get up higher."

More sparks sizzled near the tree branches. "We don't have time." Zillia grabbed an armload of lumber scraps anyway. Soonie went behind the shed and came out with a couple of wooden boxes.

Even after they'd gathered everything they could find; the stack was only a few feet high.

"We might have to convince her to jump," Wylder whispered to Zillia.

"What? Wylder, no. She'd kill herself."

"Hopefully she'd land on one of us. She might get hurt, but I don't think it's far enough for her to break her neck. We have to try something, otherwise she's going to burn to death right in front of us."

Zillia shivered. The thought was too horrible to dwell on. She made another quick search around the yard, but while there was plenty of scrap lumber and broken tools, there was nothing soft enough for the little girl to land on, not even a haystack.

Suddenly, a long, lithe shape ran from the driveway.

"Lone Warrior, what are you doing here?" gasped Soonie.

The Kiowa man didn't answer, just pushed away the pile of junk they had constructed and wrapped his arms and legs around the tree. He shimmied up the trunk, his face drawn in pain.

Despite his injury, he quickly reached the branch where Patsy sat. "All right, girl, you need to get on my back and hold on to my shoulders. Can you do that?"

"What about Feather?" came the little girl's voice.

"Here, we'll wrap her in your apron and tie it around your neck, like this. See? She's calm now. If she doesn't know what's going on, she won't be as scared."

The branches rustled violently, and then Lone Warrior slid down the trunk a few inches at a time, with Patsy clinging to his back like a frightened squirrel.

Once her feet touched the ground, she ran over to Zillia and handed her a squirming bundle. "Here's my kitty. Can we please take her to your house like you said?"

Zillia nodded and pulled the little girl into a tight hug. "Of course we can, Patsy. But why couldn't you wait until tomorrow?"

Patsy's lip trembled. "I've been so lonely without my brother and sister. And I'm kind of her family, you know? When I saw those baby kitties in the barn, I just kept thinking about how much she must miss me. I couldn't wait another day. But when I came into the house, a rat ran out and scared me. I dropped the lantern and it broke."

Words of rebuke rose to Zillia's lips, but she looked into the child's tear streaked, soot-covered face and gulped them back. "Come on, let's go home and find something for Feather to eat."

Lone Warrior and Wylder stood together, watching the flames overtake the house.

"There's nothing we can do, is there?" Zillia asked.

"No," Wylder said. As if to prove his words, the roof collapsed, and Patsy's tree burst into flames. "Fortunately, the ground is still muddy here and there are no more trees right up by the house. It's pretty likely the fire will burn itself out. However, I should ride into town and make sure the sheriff sends some folks out to keep watch."

"That would be good." Lone Warrior clutched his shoulder with his good hand. A fresh crimson stain had seeped through the bandage.

"Oh, look at you," Soonie scolded. "You opened that wound back up again. Why did you follow us when you were supposed to be resting? Even though I'm glad you did," she added.

"I was lying back in the chair, almost asleep, when a voice spoke to me, out loud. It said, "Follow your wife." I thought it was Grandpa Walt, but when I opened my eyes, no one was there. Even Grandma Louise had gone to the other room to be with the baby. I knew it was the voice of God. So I got up. I couldn't find another saddle, so I rode one of the wagon team's horses bareback. I smelled the smoke a way down the road and followed the scent here."

Wylder stared at Lone Warrior, as though seeing him for the first time. Zillia couldn't resist giving her husband a smug look.

Patsy leaned up against Zillia, her cat snuggled in her arms. "Mrs. Eckhart, can we go home now?"

"Of course, dear," said Zillia. "Let's get home before Christmas comes."

13

JOY

When Soonie woke on Christmas morning, the realization of the day rolled over her in delightful waves. She wriggled with excitement, like a puppy.

She slipped out of bed as quietly as possible so as not to disturb her still sleeping husband. Lone Warrior almost never slept through the dawn, but since his injury she'd allowed him a few more hours of shut eye. *Especially after last night.*

Kneeling beside the bed, she tucked her nightgown under her knees to protect them from the cold floor and leaned her cheek against Grandma Louise's double-wedding ring quilt.

"Lord, thank you so much that all is well. My husband and I are safe, Patsy was saved, even the cat was saved. You are so very good to us. Thank you for sending your son on Christmas. Amen."

Warm fingers touched her forehead, and she kissed her husband's hand, tears slipping down her face.

###

Soonie shuffled into the kitchen. The room was toasty warm compared to the bedroom, since she'd been too sleepy to keep up with the fire through the night. Grandma Louise already had bacon frying in one pan and a mysterious substance—perhaps pudding—in another pot on the stove.

"Merry Christmas. Can I help with something?" Soonie asked.

Grandma's smile covered her face. "Merry Christmas, dear. How about setting the table? Zillia and Wylder should be here any moment."

True to her words, the door flew open and they all blustered in. Zillia and Wylder came in first, with Margo, Orrie and Patsy. Henry and Will followed, and at the very end came Grandpa.

Everyone hugged and exchanged Christmas greetings.

In the midst of the happy chaos, Soonie noticed a tall shadow standing by the fire. She pushed through the throng until she reached her husband's side. Wrapping her fingers around his good arm, she pulled him down to whisper in his ear. "Merry Christmas, my love."

He smiled, but said nothing, his dark eyes wandering over the room.

Grandpa said a prayer, and they all sat down for a Christmas breakfast of ham, bacon, fresh bread, beans and sweet rolls. Zillia brought in a covered platter from the wagon. She pulled off the towel that covered a mysterious, lumpy shape with a flourish.

Underneath lay a rather uneven stack of roundish breads, with red candies set on the tops.

"What is that?" Orrie asked.

"Well, it's supposed to be–" Zillia began, but she was interrupted.

"Lussekater." Grandma Louise dabbed her eyes with her apron. "Sweet girl, how did you know how to make them?"

"Well, Grandpa Walt helped me." Zillia poked at one of the rolls. "They're a bit dense, but with some butter I think they'll taste all right."

Grandpa Walt grinned. "I couldn't remember all the stuff, but it looks pretty close, doesn't it?"

Grandma Louise picked a roll up and examined it. "Ah, just the sight of this bread brings back memories. My mother made it every year, and it was my job to bring the platter to the table. Thank you, Zillia, what a wonderful present."

Orrie tugged on Zillia's arm. "Is it gift time, Zillie?"

"Presents after breakfast, Orrie," said Wylder. His tone was stern, but his blue eyes danced with impatience that mirrored the little boy's.

"Everyone grab a plate and eat quick," said Grandpa Walt. "These children are getting antsy."

Soonie found it hard to sit still, despite her twenty years. *I'm so thankful we got back our saddlebags with the presents.* Her eyes met her husband's, and he gave her that special smile, the one that made her feel like the most beautiful girl in the world.

Of course, that wasn't the most important thing, but it's still nice.

Orrie grabbed the last piece of bacon and gobbled it up. "Breakfast is done." His cheeks still bulged with food. "Let's open presents!"

"All right, everyone." Grandpa rose to his feet and ambled to the other side of the room. He settled into his chair. "I've got my seat."

Grandma Louise lit the candles on the tree. They winked and flickered, each adding their own special touch to the day's perfection.

Everyone gathered around the tree, most sinking to the smooth pine floors. Will and Henry handed out the gifts.

Orrie crowed over his new wooden top and painted lead soldiers. Grandpa beamed when he opened green and white striped mittens, knitted by Grandma, and a matching muffler made by Zillia, whose handiwork had improved considerably over the years.

Grandma Louise opened Zillia's scrapbook, and a beaded shawl from Soonie.

Soonie and Zillia laughed when they opened their gifts from each other. Both held up aprons, though Zillia's was embellished with painted Comanche designs and very different from Soonie's muslin with lace trim.

An excited cry came from the children's corner, where Patsy sat. "Oh, Mrs. Eckhart! Is she really for me?"

Patsy held up Sarah, Soonie's doll. "Her hair's all fixed." The little girl touched the hem of a newly sewn dress. "She's even more beautiful than before."

"That's why I asked you to gather eggs this morning," Zillia said, mischief dancing in her eyes. "I snuck her from the room to pretty her up. The doll is from Soonie, and I made the dress."

Patsy leapt to her feet and flung her arms around Soonie. "Thank you so much! She's the only doll I've ever had, 'cept for one I made from a corn-cob once. And the rats ate her."

"Surely there weren't rats in your house?" Wylder frowned.

The little girl nodded. "Sometimes my brother fought 'em off with a stick so's they wouldn't nibble at our toes."

Soonie saw Wylder raise his eyebrows at Zillia, and Zillia nodded. *Wonder what those two are up to?*

"From your grandpa and me." Grandma handed Soonie a beautifully carved box she recognized as one that always sat on her grandparent's chest of drawers.

Soonie traced the painted flowers with a finger. "Oh, Grandma, it's lovely. I've always admired this box."

"Look inside." Grandma's eyes shone.

A red stone caught the light from a candle as Soonie opened the box. Her fingers trembled as she withdrew the garnet ring. "Your wedding ring?" she whispered. "Grandma, you can't give me this."

"Of course I can." Grandma bent down and gave her a fierce hug. "We want you to know how happy we are for you and your young man. Just wish we could have given it sooner."

Sliding the ring on her finger, Soonie blinked back tears. Grandpa gave her a proud smile from his seat by the fire.

Henry handed Wylder a bundle. "This is the last present."

Wylder unwrapped the piece of hide, bound by twine, to reveal a shining knife. Tiny birds and beasts chased each other around the bone handle.

He turned it over and over. "Who made this? I carve a little, myself, but I've never tried bone. This is beautiful."

Soonie glanced at her husband, who was playing with a piece of twine from one of the packages. "Lone Warrior made it for you," she said softly. "He was looking forward to meeting you the most."

Wylder stared down at his gift. "Thank you," he choked out. He rose and held out his hand. "Lone Warrior, I'm proud to call you my brother."

After the festivities were tidied and the youngest children put down for naps, clutching their treasures, Soonie followed Lone Warrior outside and down the path to the river, where she and

Zillia had spent so much time in their childhood. "How did you like your first white folk's Christmas?"

He squinted out at the cold, rushing water. "I enjoyed the children's laughter. And everyone seems so happy to be here. But I liked our first Christmas better."

"Huddled in a shelter with no presents, and only half a rabbit to eat?"

He pulled her closer. "But we were all alone in the open air with miles of space between us and the rest of the world. The walls are too thick here. They keep out the sky."

"As soon as you've had a few more weeks to rest, we'll go home," she promised. "But this time, we're taking the train the whole way."

That night, candles and lanterns bobbed through the streets of Bastrop as the members of the Methodist church made their way to the sacred pews and settled in for the Nativity presentation.

Children crowned with lopsided head covers and halos filed into the church. Sadie's costume, Zillia observed with relief, was free of tears and stains, and she carried the baby Jesus doll to his place in the manger with uncharacteristic gentleness.

Patsy and Orrie trooped in with the rest of the shepherds, each flashing bright smiles as they shuffled by. Wylder squeezed her hand as the organist started up the first notes of "Hark, the Herald Angels Sing!"

The play progressed smoother than Zillia ever dreamed. Her eyes kept resting on Patsy, who carried out her part with a touching seriousness.

Mrs. Fowler had told her before the play started that the little girl's grandma had taken a turn for the worst and was not likely to last the week. She'd pressed Zillia not to tell her until after Christmas. "Let the poor dear have her special day."

Zillia glanced up at Wylder, and saw that he, too, gazed at the little girl. She snuggled against his shoulder. *He'll let me keep her. We don't have much, but we can give her a family.*

The angel emerged from the shadows to deliver his message of hope and joy to the shepherds. Suddenly, Patsy's freckled face paled. She jumped to her feet, shepherd's staff clattering to the floor.

"Aunt Mel? Wade? Pearl?" she gasped.

The angel of the Lord's mouth dropped open as Patsy darted off the stage and ran down the aisle.

Zillia stood and turned to see her throw her arms around a middle-aged woman in the back pew.

"Aunt Mel, Aunt Mel, how are you? Merry Christmas! And Wade, isn't the play beautiful? Pearl, how did you all get here?"

Wade, a tall boy with dark hair and big, serious eyes, patted her on the shoulder. "Better get back up there, sis. We'll talk when your shindig's over."

"All right." Patsy ran back on stage and took her place beside Orrie. The audience laughed and clapped.

The angel of the Lord darted a wide-eyed glance at Zillia.

She nodded and mouthed the words "Go on."

The rest of the play went without a hitch and ended with a rendition of "Oh Holy Night." The song swelled over the congregation as everyone joined in, eyes closed and hands clasped before them.

Afterwards, Soonie rushed over and hugged Zillia. "You did a wonderful job! I might have to try a play at the reservation next year."

Zillia frowned. "You mean you won't be coming back next year?"

"No Zillia. We can't risk the journey again. I want to be in a place where the man I love isn't in constant danger, whether it be from bullets or misunderstanding." She nodded to where Lone Warrior stood, drinking punch and talking with Wylder and Pastor Fowler. "Until we live in a world where people can see a man's character at first glance, we must choose to stay where we're safe."

"Goodness, wouldn't that be scary. I'm not sure anyone would be safe in that case," said Zillia. "Don't we all have hidden, ugly pieces of ourselves that must be turned over to God every day?"

Someone tugged on her sleeve, and she looked down to see Patsy's soulful eyes. "Mrs. Eckhart, I want you to meet Aunt Mel."

The brown-haired woman reached out a slightly plump hand for Zillia to shake. "I can't thank you enough for taking care of my niece. My sister followed the Devil's call when she decided to run off and leave her children. I had no idea where she'd taken this one, thought she'd dragged her off along with the baby. But then I found out about their grandma being sick—my sister's first husband's mother--and decided I'd come and pay my respects. And here's our little Patsy!" she squeezed the girl's shoulders, and Patsy beamed. "Of course, I'd like to take her home with me to live with her brother and sister. My husband works with the railroad, so we can provide for them."

"Of—of course." A lump formed in Zillia's throat. But the excitement shining from Patsy's eyes was enough. *It's where she belongs. Smithville's not far away.* "We'll get your things to you as soon as possible, and your kitty, of course," she promised Patsy.

"I brought my dolly with me." Patsy pulled out Soonie's doll from the recesses of her shepherd's robe. She rushed forward and hugged Zillia. "Thank you for letting me stay with you."

The little girl pulled away and ran over to Lone Warrior, who almost dropped his punch when she wrapped her arms around his waist. "And thank you, Mr. Lone Warrior. He saved my life, you know," she said to Aunt Mel, who looked a bit alarmed.

"Oh, is that right?" Aunt Mel, eyed Lone Warrior, who had worn his braids down for the night and stood a head taller than every man in the room.

Wylder began to shoo children towards their parents, and the youngest ones began to nod off in the pews.

"It's been a wonderful Christmas," Zillia said to Soonie, as she wrapped Margo in a shawl for the ride home.

"Yes," Soonie sighed. "Maybe someday you can come and see us, in Oklahoma."

"You never know what God will put in our path," said Zillia. "But for tonight, I'm going to hold on to right now. I can't imagine a more beautiful time."

Out they went to the wagons, with the Christmas stars lighting the way home.

The End

BONUS
SHORT STORY

This is a little short story that takes place in the middle of the *of the timeline for* "The River Girl's Song," the first story in the *Texas Women of Spirit*" series. Hope you enjoy it!

The River Girl's Sanctuary

April 1888

Zillia tugged another dewberry from its thorny perch and dropped it into an already brimming basket. Spring breezes teased her brown curls, and a grasshopper leapt in front of her with a startled click.

She studied the jumbled fruit, deep purples with glimmers of red mixed in. "Should we pick more?"

Soonie gestured to the small buckboard with a slim, brown hand. "We have two empty baskets left. Grandma wants to can enough for the year. If we pick extra, my brother said Mr. Bolter will buy a few bushels to sell at the dry goods shop. Goodness knows Mr. Bolter doesn't have time to go 'gallivanting' as Grandpa Walt says, over these hills after berries"

Zillia nodded. "I could certainly use the extra money. The early vegetable crop looks promising this year, but money seems to stretch out thinner than a chicken's skin." She freed her faded calico dress from where it had snagged on a berry bush. "I'm so thankful Grandma Louise could watch Orrie for me today, I'd never have been able to gather so much."

Soonie pulled up the strings of her sunbonnet so the brim shaded her face. A rather futile action since her Comanche blood gave her skin a rich brown tint; no matter how she avoided the sun. "Grandma loves Orrie but she's just having a little more trouble keeping up with him now that he's walking so well"

Zillia sighed. "I know. Even at my age it's hard to keep up. I don't know how those chunky little legs carry him away so fast!" She wiped her forehead with the corner of her apron. "Orrie's the best little brother in the world, but he's getting braver and more reckless. Why, yesterday he climbed the ladder to the barn quicker than you could shake a stick!"

"My cousins were the same at that age. I used to have to chase them through the cornfield. Which was harder when they went two different directions." Soonie picked up a full basket of berries. "I'm taking this to the wagon. We've about emptied these bushes." She pointed through the trees. "Can you check on the other side of that thicket? I seem to remember a nice patch over there."

"All right." Zillia pushed through the copse of trees, keeping a careful eye out for the snakes that slithered around the berry bushes to catch the mice. *Last thing I need is a snake bite. Then Orrie really would have no one.* She swallowed the lump that always formed in her throat when she imagined Orrie alone. Babies without families went to orphanages and children's homes in the big city of Austin. Horrible places, most of them, where the girls and boys were beaten for minor infractions and made to do manual labor all day. She'd heard that most of the children looked like little scarecrows, with barely enough to eat. *We might not have much, but Orrie has never gone hungry. I'd go from door to door begging before I let that happen.*

She wormed her way through the trees. The riverbank was only a few yards away, and the sound of the rushing water poured through the trees. A bank of earth, covered in dark purple berries, rose up before her.

"Soonie, come see all of these!" she shouted.

Soonie rushed through the forest, two empty baskets swinging from her hands. "Perfect," she breathed.

Zillia picked her way around the hill, but as she came to the other side, she stopped short. Beneath thick overhand of vegetation were gaps of darkness. She stuck her hand through and felt . . . nothing.

"Soonie, have you ever been back here?"

Soonie paused. "Can't say that I have."

"Well, you should see this. It's so covered in vines, I almost missed it."

Zillia used a stick to sweep away the curtain of dewberry brambles. Under a thin layer of earth, the bank was rock, and the side of that rock was hollowed out. The sunlight revealed a perfect little room, high enough to stand in and wide enough for both girls to comfortably sit.

Soonie ducked inside. "This is fun." Her voice echoed on the walls.

"Yep." Zillia brushed away dirt and leaves and sat on a smooth rock. "I wonder if Indians used this hideout? I wish we'd known about this place when we were little girls."

"Me too." Soonie settled herself down on another rock. "Look here." She poked the dirt with her stick. "This must have been a fire pit once. I think you're right. Someone used it as a shelter. Maybe years ago."

Zillia surveyed the room. "Well, we might not be children anymore, but I think I'll come back here sometimes. Not too far from the house and it's the perfect place to come when I need to think."

Soonie nudged her shoulder. "Even with Orrie?"

Zillia folded her arms and leaned back. "I think he'll love it."

###

Wylder loaded the last basket into the wagon. "These should sell nicely. You'll probably get $2.00 a bushel." Removing his floppy wide-brimmed hat, he pushed back his unruly brown curls. "Hot day for April. I'll have to hurry these up so they won't spoil on the way."

"I hadn't thought of that." Zillia tapped her chin as she considered the brimming baskets. Even with Grandma Louise taking a portion of their plunder, they'd had six bushels left.

Grandma Louise came out of the house, shaking flour from her apron. "Orrie's still asleep. Henry plumb wore him out playing hide and seek in the barn. He's been good as gold today."

"He always behaves for Henry." Zillia smiled.

Wylder gestured to the baskets. "Grandma, we need to keep these berries cool all the way to town. Have any ideas?".

Grandma Louise peeked into the back of the wagon, wisps of thin white hair sticking to her face. "Well, now. Maybe flap at 'em with a cloth dipped in cool water from the well? Or place 'em in buckets of water."

"Don't think buckets of water would be practical." Wylder rubbed his chin. "But you might have something with the cool cloths."

"We could wrap cloths around the baskets as well," suggested Soonie. "The only problem is, I can't go to town. There's a basketful of mending to do before Sunday. Those boys are rough on their trousers and they're down to last year's high waters."

Zillia picked up a berry and allowed to roll around in her hand. "I could go, if Orrie stays asleep."

Grandma Louise waved a towel. "Go on. You won't make any money from the berries if they dry up like prunes on the way to town."

"We'll hurry back." Zillia popped the berry in her mouth, allowing the sweet-tart juices to roll over her tongue.

"Shall I help you up?" Wylder took Zillia's hands and swung her up into the buckboard. A friend 'close as a brother,' he'd done this a hundred times. But today he didn't let go right away, and his gaze held her own a bit longer than normal. A new light sparked in the center of the deep umber, something she couldn't read.

Wonder what's going on with him? Wylder always got ancy in the spring. Maybe he's tired of being stuck in a small cabin with all these kids.

"Get to fanning." Wylder hopped up on the front seat and jiggled the reigns.

Zillia tucked several moist cloths around the bushel baskets. She grabbed the largest one and began to flap it over the tops, sending a breeze over them.

"I feel so silly," she giggled. "I hope we don't pass anyone we know."

"Oh well," Wylder shouted over the rumble of the wagon wheels. "Everyone 'round here loves dewberries. They'll probably set up a plaque in tribute to your noble deeds at the town hall."

"Now you're talking foolishness." Zillia flapped the cloth harder.

Zillia continued to fan the berries for the thirty minute trip to town. By the time they arrived on Bastrop's Main Street, her arms ached.

The wagon rumbled to a stop in front of the general store. Wylder rested his elbows against the edge of the wagon. "They look good to me. I'll remember your skills if I ever need wind for a ship." He jumped down and tied the horse to the hitching post. Pointing to a line of farmers winding out the door, he said, "Quite a few people waiting. I'm guessing with early spring crops, everyone's checking their luck with Mr. Bolter."

"Yes, it could be a while." Zillia sighed.

Wylder jabbed his thumb at a building a few doors down. "The blacksmith's been repairing a bridle for me. Said it'd probably be finished by today. Would you mind asking him about it? I'll wait in line here."

"Fine with me." Zillia was glad to escape standing in the stuffy shop's entry way. She'd never been overly fond of crowds and the farmers straight from hot fields and barns were certain to bring less than desirable odors with them. *Not that I smell like a rose myself.* This morning she'd mucked out the stable and cleaned the goat's scrap buckets before she'd gone berry picking.

Fortunately, there was no line in front of the smithy.

Zillia made her way up the creaking front steps. The sound of metal crashing against metal rang through the air. Smoke stung her eyes, and the smells of coal and dust and iron swept into her senses.

She'd almost reached the door when something tugged at her shirtwaist. "Miss Zillia, please, can you help?" A little boy , just a few years older than Orrie, looked up at her with pleading eyes.

Hezekiah Trent. The grandson of Jemimah Trent, who was Orrie's grandmother and the horrible matriarch of the Trent tribe.

"Please come with me," the youngster said again. His clothes were torn, and his face was covered with dirt. He almost looked like those children from the poor houses she'd pictured earlier.

Suspicion rose up within her. Zillia had never seen a Trent up to anything but bad news. "Where's your father, Hezekiah?" She raised her hand to shield her eyes and peered down the street.

"He's gone, Miss. Please come with me. I need you real bad."

She sighed and darted a glance at the dry goods store. Wylder had disappeared inside, so there was no way to get his attention.

"Alright Hezekiah, but let's hurry. I don't want Wylder to wonder where I am."

The little boy darted down the steps across the street and into the bushes that grew along the side of the bank building.

"Hezekiah, what on earth?" Zillia hurried after him as fast as she was able, gathering up her thick skirts to keep them off the dirty lane.

She pushed through the bushes. *Where is he?* "Hezekiah?" Her voice carried through the small clearing in the midst of a group of cedar trees.

"Over here!" came a muffled voice.

Branches cracked as she quickened her pace, then the ground gave way beneath her feet. She found herself falling down, down, into darkness. Roots pulled at her skin and fingernails tore as she clawed at the sides of the pit on the way down.

She landed in a thick layer of mud with a jolt. Sharp pains stabbed into her right ankle.

Dazed, she struggled to stand. Her ankle would not allow it, and she sank down to her knees.

Three children's faces appeared at the top of the pit, some ten feet above her.

"Ha ha," Hezekiah's voice floated down. "That's what you get for stealing from my family."

Zillia sighed and shook her head. "I'm not a thief, Hezekiah. The farm is rightfully mine. Mama never signed it over to Jeb." *Why am I trying to explain myself to a six-year-old?*

"Stealer!" Hezekiah shouted. "You can stay down there your whole life!" The children disappeared.

"Don't leave me here! Go get an adult!" Zillia shouted after them. But they were gone.

Oh, God. Zillia put her head in her hands. *How could I have forgotten about this sinkhole?* The pit had been there for years. Once upon a time, a fence had been built around it to keep this very thing from happening but over the years it had fallen apart, never to be replaced.

Her ankle throbbed. Please God, don't let it be broken. I have so much to do with the spring harvesting and planting. Please. Let someone find me.

"Help!" she yelled. "Someone help!"

Her words were absorbed by the earthen walls. *Can anyone even hear me?*

Water seeped through her skirt. Her nose wrinkled. *I thought I smelled bad before.*

She yelled a few more times, then leaned against the wall. The pain was becoming almost too much to bear. Her stomach rumbled. She hadn't eaten anything but a few berries since breakfast.

After a few more attempts to struggle to her feet, she gave up. Resting her head on her arms, she fell into a fitful sleep.

"Zillia! Zillia! Wake up!" The voice filtered into her dreams.

"Mama?" she said groggily. She opened her eyes. The daylight that had filtered in from the top of the pit was gone. Stars peppered the entrance.

"Mama?" Zillia gazed around her. Of course, it couldn't be. Mama had been gone for almost two years; she'd died the day Orrie had come into the world.

"Orrie. Oh, I have to get out of here. I have to take care of him." Zillia grasped a root in the wall and pulled herself up again.

Her ankle was so swollen it felt like it would burst through her shoe, but it supported her weight.

I can do this. I can figure a way out.

Gritting her teeth, she felt along the sides for more of the roots that had torn her skin on the way down. A thick one held true. The pit was narrow, and she was able to rest her back on one side while pushing with her feet on the other side.

Using roots as a support, she made her way up one agonizing foot, then another.

Invisible flames surrounded her ankle, creeping up her leg, and her waterlogged skirts added unwanted weight, but she continued.

Almost there . . . Inches from the top, the mouth of the pit widened. Her fingers scrabbled for another root, a rock, anything to pull up a tiny bit further.

"God, please, please!" she cried, out loud this time.

"Zillia!" A female voice, not her mother. Real, true, and hovering over the hole.

Please, please. She braced herself against the crumbling wall and shouted with all her strength. "Here!"

Twigs and branches rustled overhead, and torchlight flooded into her eyes. "Zillia?" Soonie's concerned face popped into view. "Oh, Zillia! We thought we'd never find you!" Soonie yelled over her shoulder. "She's here! Over here!"

"Hurry, Soonie, I'm slipping!"

"Oh goodness, of course. I'm going to lay flat on the ground here. Give me a minute." Soonie disappeared, and Zillia figured she was placing her torch in the earth. A moment later she was back, her strong hands gripping Zillia's arms.

"I think . . . I can pull you up. I can at least keep you from sliding," Soonie gasped.

Zillia shoved her feet against the wall to help Soonie. But the opening was too wide. "I can't make it," she panted. "My ankle hurts. I'm going to fall back down."

"No you're not." Wylder reached down and grasped Zillia's shoulders.

Tingles ran down her shoulder blades and she sagged with instant relief.

With a giant heave, brother and sister pulled her out of the pit.

Thick grass cooled Zillia's cheek as she lay, gasping on the ground.

Wylder smoothed her hair from her forehead and looked her over, his brow furrowed. "Are you hurt? You said something about your ankle."

"I think it'll be okay," said Zillia.

"How on earth did you fall down there?" Soonie asked.

"The Trent kids. Covered it up and lured me over here."

"Those little scamps. Wouldn't be surprised if Able put 'em up to it." Wylder scowled. "We've been looking for you all day. A lady in town said she thought she'd seen you head for home. I was surprised you'd left without me but I knew you were anxious to get back to Orrie. When I got to the cabin and you weren't there, we started searching the path on the way back."

"The town's been looking for you for hours," Soonie said.

"I'm sorry everyone went to so much trouble," Zillia rested back in the grass. Pinpricks of pain ran up her arms from her raw hands.

"Let's look at that ankle." Soonie tugged at her shoe. "Goodness, I think we might need to cut this away." She drew a knife from a sheath on her belt and began hacking at the leather.

"Oh, I can't afford a new pair of shoes," Zillia groaned.

"I have a pair I outgrew before I wore them out." Soonie pulled away pieces of leather.

Though her fingers were gentle, every movement brought new jolts of pain.

Soonie shook her head. "The doc's out looking tonight. I'm going to wait for him before I mess with this anymore."

Wylder waved his lantern through the trees. "Over here!" he called.

Clusters of lights bobbed in answer.

He knelt beside Zillia. "Everyone will be glad you're safe." He smoothed her tangled hair back from her forehead. "I'm glad your safe." His voice was so quiet Zillia almost didn't catch the words.

A few weeks later, Zillia headed back to the forest clearing. Her ankle had been turned badly, but after a few days of rest the pain had almost gone. Now she only hobbled a little.

Hezekiah had been questioned about the pit, but he swore up and down he didn't know it was there. His grandmother had given him a good scolding in front of the townspeople, but Zillia had seen her slip Hezekiah a licorice stick on the side. *I'll never trust a Trent again, that's for sure.*

She and Orrie slipped through the thicket, wading through knee-high wildflowers that perfumed the air with their sweet, powdery fragrance.

Orrie's chubby fingers were wrapped around her hand and he bounced beside her, a grin covering his freckled face. Occasionally he would jabber about something he saw on the path in his own baby language, sprinkled with an intelligible word or two. "Zillie, rock! Zillie, bug!"

"I know." She ruffled his mop of blond curls. "There's lots of fun things to see, Orrie."

Finally they came to the bank she'd found before. She pushed away the overgrowth and led him inside.

"Oooh, Zillie. Dark."

"I know, Orrie. But look how nice!"

The smooth stones had been covered with old shawls Zillia recognized from Soonie and Wylder's house. A pile of firewood had been stacked against one wall, and the fire pit had been cleaned. A basket resided in the corner. When Zillia peeped in, she saw a tin of crackers, a small tinder box, and a jar of . . ."

"Dewberry preserves! Oh, Orrie, Soonie must have stocked this up as a surprise!"

She started a little fire in the pit to chase out the spring dampness, and she and Orrie sat down to a little feast of crackers and jam.

As they munched in contentment, Zillia bowed her head. "God, even in my crazy life, I thank you for moments like these. For me just to be. You truly are my shelter in the storm."

About the Author

Angela Castillo has lived in Bastrop, Texas, home of the River Girl, almost her entire life. She studied Practical Theology at Christ for the Nations in Dallas. She lives in Bastrop with her husband and three children. Angela has written several short stories and books, including *the Toby the Trilby* series for kids. to find out more about her writing, go to
http://angelacastillowrites.weebly.com

Manufactured by Amazon.ca
Bolton, ON